To M

LUGER

...ter + wishes

WILLIAM KINREAD

William

Fisher King Publishing

LUGER

Published by
Fisher King Publishing
The Studio
Arthington Lane
Pool in Wharfedale
LS21 1JZ
England
www.fisherkingpublishing.co.uk

To my wife Claire
and my son Toby

Chapter One

January 1945 – The Ardennes

Talent is usually a blessing. He felt his was a curse. Destined to destroy rather than create, John Field was a sniper. Not just a sniper but an outstanding marksman renowned in the Royal Marines and a personal favourite of Field Marshal Bernard Montgomery who knew he could be relied upon to finish the task in hand. He had been used to delay the German advance on Dunkirk. He had dozens of kills in the North African desert and now as the Allies advanced towards the industrial heartland of Germany once again, he was picking off the pre-eminent targets.

He was not one of the boys. Ordinary troops were suspicious of snipers. They thought snipers were cold-blooded killers. How little did they know. They did not see him lying awake at night; they did not see the involuntary shaking and they described him as bad-tempered when really, they had just caught him unawares while experiencing a flashback.

John Field was a Quantity Surveyor before the War

interrupted his career. He was precise and he was precise about his killing. Wasn't this better than blanket bombing? Better than artillery fire? He did not kill indiscriminately; nor unknowingly and there were no civilian casualties. He killed key people in an effort to win the War; to achieve the strategic initiative; to protect his fellow soldiers. He was entwined in a battle of good versus evil but somehow, he didn't feel very good.

"Ready, Doug?"

"Ready." Doug Parker was the closest thing he had to a friend. Not quite as tall as Field and not as strikingly handsome but broad and strong. He could carry weights that made others buckle and he never gave up. In the heat of battle, he was definitely a man you wanted on your side and today they were working as a pair.

"Have you heard they've re-named us?" Doug said. "We are now part of first Commando Brigade."

"I know," John replied. "They're always messing about with titles. I've been called all sorts of things!"

Doug laughed.

"But it doesn't matter. They had to change Special Service Brigade because the initials SS reminded people of the Nazis but at the end of the day, we're still Green Berets." He kissed the globe on his Royal Marine Beret Badge.

The Green Beret was only issued once you had passed selection and training and the basic training was almost three times longer than that of the regular army. That automatically made the Royal Marines better prepared, but the training was also much tougher. It was designed to push physical and mental strengths to the limits of endurance. So, when the Green Beret was presented at the passing out parade, there was a feeling of immense pride; the recruits had been tested and they had persevered.

"Yes. Unloved by the Army because we're in the Navy and unloved by the Navy because we're not sailors."

"It's just jealousy old boy. They know we're the best. Come on we'd better go."

Intelligence had been received from local Belgian partisans that a German officer and possibly his driver had got cut off during the Allies counteroffensive and were held up in a farmhouse keeping an elderly farmer and his wife hostage. They had advanced with the fifth Panzer Army to some woods South of Foy-Notre-Dame in Belgium and then as the Allies pushed back, they had become stuck behind enemy lines. Field and Parker were tasked with sorting it out.

John showed Doug the map.

"If the intelligence is correct, they are about a mile to the West of us. We will move about half a mile towards them and then head South along this track and then through the woods to the river Lesse. Then we follow the river westwards until we are half a mile beyond the farmhouse. Then we take a right going in a Northerly direction. This will take us half a mile behind the farmhouse but on higher ground. Finally, we head back East to this copse at the rear of the farmhouse." He prodded the map. "It's an elevated position about 300 yards away."

It was still dark, and the landscape was covered in snow. It was about two feet deep and big blobs of it covered the branches of the conifer trees weighing them down. Some of the smaller trees were so over-laden they looked as though they were bowing in deference as the snipers approached. They needed to be in position by sunrise and they had about three miles to trek to reach their destination.

They were wearing snowsuits made from villagers' bedsheets, but they were for camouflage, not warmth. The snowsuits quickly absorbed moisture, so they froze stiff and crackled as Field and Parker trudged through the snow. The cold air cut through their uniforms with the ease of a knife through butter, however, they were used to hardship and they would be fine as long as they kept moving. Field just didn't want to be lying in position for too long.

They walked along a forest track until they reached the river. It looked black against the white snow.

Nature is so beautiful, Field thought.

The river acted as their guide until they had to turn North, at which point an owl hooted as dawn started to break.

"Goodnight," John said back to it as owls are nocturnal or was it wishing us good luck?

Then they started to climb, and their breath became shorter as the cold air chilled their lungs. Even though they were cold, mild perspiration moistened their brows and then cooled the skin as it made contact with the air.

The copse was perfectly situated. Twenty or so mature larch trees grown on the top of a rocky outcrop but not too close together. John and Doug crouched behind a tree to get their bearings. They could position themselves at either side of the copse using the protection of the trees but still have a clear view.

A stone farmhouse nestled about 300 yards away, about 100 feet below them. It was long and low with a grey slate roof and blue wooden shutters on the windows. It probably had three rooms in a row but was only one room deep. It was a common design for a farmhouse. A larger barn was set at right angles to the farmhouse and it had a large central entrance in the form of an open archway. There was a cobbled courtyard between the farmhouse and the barn with a water pump and a large stone water trough. It formed quite a feature. Along the northern boundary was the forest. West to East was pasture and that would be the direction of their shots. To the South a single-track road which ran to the next village.

They would be looking towards the sun as it rose in the East, but the skies were grey; they didn't think it would pose a problem. Luckily there was no wind. Snipers don't like the wind.

"Do you see that?" John said, pointing at a Tiger II tank partially concealed in the barn.

"I do and I know what it means," Doug replied.

Strangely, Belgian intelligence was obviously inaccurate. A Tiger II tank should have a Commander, a driver, a gunner and a loader and possibly a radio operator although given the losses the Germans had suffered on the Russian front the Commander probably worked the radio. That meant that unless someone had been killed, they could have four or five targets to deal with and they were not meant to get into a shooting match. That could mean collateral damage.

"Let's get into position and see what transpires," John suggested.

Doug took the North end of the copse and John the South.

The grey dawn light was breaking at around 08.00 hours when a young soldier came out of the farmhouse. His name was Hans. He was in uniform but couldn't be more than eighteen years old. In the last throws of the War, the German front line troops were getting younger and younger as they replaced their fallen colleagues. He won't have had much training and looked as though he only weighed ten and a half stone. He was carrying a radio and he sat on the water trough as he started to synchronise it. This posed a dilemma for John and Doug. They were under orders to take out the highest-ranking officers first but second in priority was always the radio operator. The last thing you wanted was someone calling for help or revealing what was going on.

John signalled to Doug to wait. He wanted to see if anyone else came out. He also didn't really want to shoot such a junior soldier. John and Doug had been twenty-three when they signed up and after six years, John was getting tired of killing. Somehow this kid just didn't look like fair game.

SS-Hauptsturmfuhrer Manfred Fuchs burst out of the farmhouse swearing expletives. He strode over to Hans and pulling his Luger out of its holster, he struck the lad across the side of his face knocking him to the ground.

"Dummkopf!" He screamed. "Do you want to give our position away?"

The initial success of the German advance during the Ardennes Offensive was down to two things. Firstly, following the attempt on his life the previous July, Hitler had become more and more paranoid about the trustworthiness of the Wehrmacht and so, for the Ardennes Offensive, he had relied heavily on his own Waffen-SS which was why Fuchs had been assigned to the 2nd Panzer Division from the elite Leibstandarte SS Adolf Hitler (LSSAH). Secondly, the advance had been a complete surprise to the Allies because fighting from their heartland meant the Germans could rely on their extensive telephone and telegraph networks, so radios were hardly necessary. This meant no enciphered messages to be decrypted by the codebreakers at Bletchley Park. The Allies simply hadn't got wind of the German plans.

"Sorry, sorry," Hans said. "I was just trying to find out where our Division was so we could work out how to join them."

"That's for me to decide!" Fuchs shouted. Hans had half picked himself up and was kneeling now, but Fuchs lashed out again this time kicking him in the crotch.

Manfred Fuchs had a high opinion of himself. Over the last year he had been awarded the Knight's Cross of the Iron Cross with Oak Leaves. In January 1944 he was awarded the Knight's Cross for achieving the destruction of 100 enemy tanks over the previous three years mainly on the Eastern Front. Then in June 1944, the Oak Leaves had been added for the destruction of twelve tanks and eight personnel carriers at a battle in the countryside South of Bayeux. The award was presented to him by Adolf Hitler personally at the Wolf's Lair near Rastenburg, his eastern front headquarters. It would be a bit embarrassing to admit, therefore, that his tank crew was in its current plight simply because he had run out of fuel.

Fuchs was also stressed. He had secretly tried the radio himself the night before and feared he may have already compromised their position, but he could see no way out. They were stuck behind enemy lines with no means of escape and so the sensible thing to do would be to surrender but Hitler's orders were strictly against this. Hitler expected his Army to make a last stand and this was especially so of the SS. Fuchs had lapped up the propaganda and enjoyed the status of being a panzer ace even though he knew most of his 'kills' on the Eastern Front had been with superior equipment against an untrained enemy and for his more recent act of valour, he had simply ambushed the Allies from behind when the road ahead was blocked by a broken-down vehicle. Now, therefore, fame was demanding its price.

He knew though that the War was lost. Everyone knew it was lost and if he did surrender who would be around to reprimand him? There were rumours, however, that there was a bounty on his head. He had dismissed them as a joke, but someone had been asking questions. Perhaps, the Allies had seen the propaganda in which case he could be a marked man and surrender could mean a trial, prison or even execution.

John signalled Doug to get into position. Lying with his legs apart and resting on his elbows Field tucked the Lee-Enfield .303 into his shoulder. It was just a workhorse. The same standard rifle that all the soldiers were issued with except this No. 4 Mk 1 (T) had a wooden cheekpiece and a telescopic sight.

Fuchs was looking now towards the copse as he

contemplated his options. Field could see the short dark hair flecked with grey either side of his head and his eyes which looked too close together. He had a slim build but loose flesh under his chin.

He's not a strong man, Field thought.

Field lined up the crosshairs between the eyes. They marked a cross down the nose and across the eyebrows.

Ironic, he thought.

It was an easy shot. Field had trained in Scotland where he was made to crawl to within fifty yards of a stag before being allowed to shoot. He had trained in the dessert where allowances had to be made for the wind and, because of the open terrain, shots taken at long distances. This shot had no such complexities. He exhaled slowly and squeezed the trigger. He heard the crack of the shot, felt the recoil and watched Fuchs collapse instantly as though his legs had been taken from under him.

The blue door of the farmhouse flung open and a man in a vest ran out carrying a machine gun. He was bald with a big fat face and his belly was hanging over his grey army trousers. Doug had him marked and fired. The bullet threw him back before he had fully got through the doorway. Another soldier followed, stepping over the body. He was fully dressed and started firing randomly. He was wearing a helmet, so Field lowered the sights and shot him in the neck. Again, he fell instantly but the bullet must have severed the carotid artery as blood started squirting violently from the gaping wound.

Hans was still by the water trough. He had been crouched behind it but now he stood up holding his hands in the air.

"Don't shoot. Don't shoot," he shouted. He looked scared out of his wits. Doug looked across at John questioningly, but John shook his head.

"Keep me covered," he said. "I'll go down."

John Field walked towards the farmhouse carrying his rifle at his side. He looked relaxed. He realised that if Hans wanted to reach for his pistol, he would be able to take a shot before he could do anything about it but he also knew that Doug would have Hans in his crosshairs and the slightest wrong move would be his last. Perhaps, Hans appreciated Field looked relaxed for a reason because he simply stood there with his hands held high.

An elderly couple inched gingerly out of the doorway. They were holding on to each other and looked in shock.

"Keep your hands up." Field said to Hans as he walked into the courtyard.

By the time Field had walked from the copse to the farmhouse, the soldier with the neck wound had stopped twitching and bled to death.

"Rope?" Field said, looking at the elderly couple. He made a gesture with his hands and then said, "corde," remembering some French from he knew not where.

The old man scurried off and came back with a piece

of rope that looked as though it had been cut off a cow's halter.

"Merci," he said. That much French he could remember from school.

He tied Hans's hands behind his back as tightly as he could and sat him on the water trough telling him to stay put. Hans got the message.

John went over to Fuchs's body and ripped the dog tag from his neck. HQ wanted the identity of all officers killed. Then he picked up the Luger. He had always wanted one and this was his prize. It was the most beautiful pistol ever made. The angled grip resulting in the back of the action resting nicely on that soft skin between the thumb and forefinger made it superbly balanced. He took the holster from Fuchs's belt and looked for ammunition. The Luger would be no good without it.

Then he noticed his watch. It was a Rolex Oyster.

What a stroke of luck, he thought as he undid the strap and slipped it into his pocket.

Field then checked the inside pockets of Fuchs's jacket, looking for his wallet. Finding it, he tugged at it anxiously and, again, slipped it into his own pocket.

Lost in the moment, he had been oblivious to his surroundings but suddenly he became aware that he was being watched by the farmer and his wife who were staring at him in dismay.

John quickly stood up and with his rifle in his left hand

and the Luger in his right, he waved both arms at Doug signalling him to come down.

"You will be all right now," John said to the farmer. "We will let the authorities know about the bodies."

When Doug arrived, John pointed the Luger at Hans and told him to get up.

"At least we can take the short route back to base," Doug said.

With Hans walking in front of them, they soon covered the mile back to their encampment.

"They've got a live one." The voice of Lieutenant Colonel Alan Skinner boomed across the camp. He cut an impressive figure. Six foot three inches tall with angular features and a well-defined nose. Always insulting his men in a camaraderie sort of way he was a popular and fair leader but having come up through the ranks he realised the importance of being politically astute and he always made sure he gave his superiors what they wanted.

"Yes sir, and three dead," John said.

He pulled the dog tag out of his pocket.

"It was a stranded tank crew. This one was an officer."

"Manfred Fuchs." Lieutenant Colonel Skinner said reading the tag. "That name rings a bell. Well done. Go and get some breakfast. We'll deal with this urchin."

John Field lay on his bunk, letting his breakfast go down. He looked at the watch. It was steel with a brown leather strap. It had a cream dial with Arabic numerals except where the number six should be there was a subsidiary dial indicating the seconds. The large Arabic numbers were toffee coloured and luminous as were the hands. A second smaller set of numbers marked the twenty-four-hour clock in red.

What a beauty, John thought as he turned it over in his hand. Engraved on the back, it said, 'To my Freddie, always yours, Judith.'

A lump stuck in John's throat. He put the watch in a tin of his belongings and opened the wallet. It contained identity papers, a driving license, some Reichsmarks and a photograph of a woman and child.

Was this Judith? He wondered. The child was a boy, perhaps four or five years old. John couldn't tell. He wasn't good with ages. He let out a large sigh and threw the wallet in his tin box. Suddenly his prizes had just lost their attraction.

A young adjutant knocked on the door and entered the office of Colonel Lord Jeremy Granville at MOD headquarters in London.

"Excuse me, sir. I have a delivery for you." He handed him a padded brown envelope.

Granville looked up from his desk and took the envelope in his right hand.

"Thank you. You may go."

Granville opened the envelope and looked at the 'With

Compliments' slip. It simply said, 'with regards from Lt Col Skinner.'

Granville emptied the contents into his hand. It was a dog tag. He read the inscription, 'Manfred Fuchs,' clenched his fist and smiled.

Chapter Two

March 1987 – North Yorkshire

The wound was massive. It went from behind the shoulder, under the armpit and up the side of his chest in a large semi-circle. John Field looked at it in dismay. It was bigger than he thought. Even the stitches were big, and the blood had congealed around the knots. His flesh was already starting to colour, yellow and purple and the whole area was washed in a yellow staining anti-septic.

Years of smoking had taken their toll. When the cancer was diagnosed, he was advised that the left lung had to be removed but this surgery was more extensive than he had imagined.

He had been operated on the day before, came around from the anaesthetic, then drifted in and out of sleep. Yesterday evening a nurse had checked he was able to urinate, and he was given something to eat but, other than that, he hadn't seen anyone for hours. Suddenly he realised he needed to pee.

John pressed the alarm button, but no one came. He had not waited long. He was known as being bad-tempered, although irritable would be a better description.

John rolled on to his right side and managed to push himself up into a sitting position. He was sat well back and his feet didn't quite touch the floor.

I can do this, he thought. I am a Royal Marine. He dropped off the bed onto the floor, wobbled and steadied himself on the iron bed frame. Gently, with bare feet, he shuffled towards the washroom.

He was desperate now. He scurried past a bath with a hoist above it and made it to the toilet. He leant his right hand on the wall below the cistern and; sweet relief.

What John didn't realise is that urinating first thing in the morning rapidly lowers the blood pressure. He felt woozy, started to sway and his vision went black and white. He remembered seeing his urine spray up against the wall, a falling sensation and that was it. The next thing he became aware of was the commotion. A nurse bent over him and others were shouting instructions.

John had fallen against the bath, hitting his wound on its enamel corner. He lay in a pool of blood and urine and his pyjamas were soaking wet.

Somehow, he ended up back on his bed, his pyjama jacket removed, and a sheet tied around his chest. It was already stained red with blood.

"We've called your consultant, Mr Field." The nurse said. "He will get here as soon as he can, and you will have to go into surgery this afternoon. Your wound will need to be re-stitched."

John was out of breath. It was an effort to breathe. He was sweating but cold – a sure sign that the body was in shock.

"What time is it?" He asked.

"It's 8.30 AM. We will get you cleaned up and then into theatre as soon as we can."

"Call my solicitor, please. I need to make a Will. The number is easy to remember. It's 565565. Ryders. The solicitor's name is Ronnie Roberts."

Ian Sutherland was in the post room when Ronnie Roberts walked in.

"Hello. How are we?" Ronnie said to him.

"Well, thank you." Ian replied, thinking to himself, why does he always use the royal 'We'?

It was Ian's first week at Ryders, the largest firm of solicitors in Harrogate but still quite a parochial outfit compared with the Leeds firm where Ian had just finished his Articles.

Ronnie Roberts was a partner and the third generation of Roberts to join Ryders.

Obviously, the patriarch was a Ryder who founded the firm in 1912. He had been joined by Ronnie's grandfather within a year, but the firm had already been named by then and the founding father wasn't inclined to change it.

The Ryders were clever, quietly spoken, astute people,

from middle-class backgrounds. Politically liberal and open-minded. The Roberts were not. They were upper-middle-class, right-wing and many of their opinions were prejudiced.

Traditionally, every Roberts' male had to have a Christian name beginning with an 'R' and unfortunately for Ronnie, by the time it came to his turn, all the decent names had gone.

Historically, the Roberts had made their money as stockbrokers in Hong Kong. For the last seventy-five years, this had ensured a public-school education for all the male offspring, although none had ever managed to get to University. Ronnie had qualified as a solicitor by working in the family business and sitting and re-sitting the exams as he went along.

Ronnie was a short man, a little plump and nervous of any work that was the least bit complicated or contentious.

"We've just had a call from Harrogate Hospital," he said. "One of my clients needs a death bed Will. John Field's his name. Now, run along will you."

"What, now?" Ian asked in a surprised voice.

Ronnie looked at him but did that strange thing with his eyes which he always did when he was facing confrontation or felt nervous. He rolled them upwards so that the iris disappeared behind his eyelids and you could only see the whites of his eyes.

"Yes, now. He could be about to die."

Ian grabbed a pad of paper and hurried to the car park. He paused momentarily, to admire his light metallic blue Jaguar E-type and then opened the driver's door. Being six foot two, it was not the easiest car to squeeze into so Ian had to sit in it first, then lift up his knees and swing around to the front before stretching his legs down the tunnel to the pedals.

The E-type was a 3.8-litre roadster, two-seater convertible with a straight six-cylinder engine and chrome spoked-wire wheels. Ian's father had bought it in 1962 and just used it on sunny days but he died in 1977 when Ian was just sixteen years old. He left it to Ian in his Will, but, for insurance purposes, the vesting date of the gift was postponed until Ian was twenty-five. It had, therefore, been in storage for the best part of a decade and was still in immaculate condition. Ian loved it, for sentimental as well as aesthetic reasons and agreed with Enzo Ferrari who had said that it was the most beautiful car ever made.

Ian started the engine and with that familiar roar ringing in his ears, headed for the hospital, which was just a couple of miles away. His mind was racing. He had spent six months doing nothing but Wills in the Leeds firm during his Articles, but he had never before done a death bed Will. He would have to hand-write it and find a second witness, so he went over the standard clauses in his head.

Yes, I know them off by heart, he reassured himself.

Arriving at the hospital, Ian asked the receptionist the name of the ward and then set off to find it. He walked down a long corridor, then, as his anxiety level started to rise, he ran up some stairs. Then back along another corridor which seemed to be in the opposite direction to that from which he had just come. Eventually, he found the ward and entering through swing doors, looked for the Sister in charge.

"Hello. I am Ian Sutherland from Ryders," he said. "I've come to see John Field."

"Oh, yes. He's just through there. Beth will take you."

A pretty nurse with short dark hair and petite figure gave him a smile. She had a name badge with Elizabeth on it. Briefly, Ian was lost for words. Only for a second or two, but it felt like an age.

"Thanks," he said, feeling rather embarrassed.

Beth walked him to John's bedside. John was sitting up. Ian noticed his full head of hair was still dark for someone of his age although it was streaked with grey and he had large brown eyes. The top sheet was pulled up to the bottom of his chin.

"Hello. I'm Ian Sutherland from Ryders. I'm afraid Mr Roberts is engaged so he asked me to come on his behalf." Ian held out his hand and John gave him a firm handshake. Both men appreciated the affirmation.

"Right, I'll leave you two to get on then," Beth said in a soft Scottish accent.

Ian turned back to look at her.

"Yes, thank you very much."

"Moves like a gazelle, doesn't she?" John said, taking Ian by surprise.

"Yes, she is very striking," Ian replied after a short pause. They had already made a connection.

"I'm glad you've come. That Roberts is an idiot. Tell me, does he still do that funny thing with his eyes?"

"Yes, he does," Ian said, laughing. "Now, I understand you would like a Will?"

"Yes, I'm afraid I've never got around to making one."

"Is this something you want me to write out now or would you just like to give me instructions and I will come back when it is typed up?" Ian's voice trailed off as he realised what he had just asked.

John pulled back the top sheet and revealed his bare chest tied together with blood-soaked bandages. Ian looked away quickly.

"Better get on with it; just in case."

"Right, what would you like to do?"

"I just want to leave everything to my two children."

"You're not married then?" Ian asked.

"I divorced my first wife and soon afterwards, she died of cancer. My children blame me because they think the cancer was brought on by the stress of the divorce. I then remarried but my second wife has recently left me and now she wants a divorce. I'm not the easiest person to live with."

"Your second wife could make a claim against your estate," Ian advised.

"She'll get the house," John replied. "It's in joint names."

"Do we have your deeds?"

"Yes. You have everything."

"Good. I will check the house is held as what we call joint tenants, sorry about the legal language, which means your second wife will inherit your half share automatically. Who do you want as your Executors?"

"Can I have my children?" John asked.

"Yes, of course. What are their names?"

"My son is Edward Field, although we call him Ted and my daughter is Janet Mitchell."

"No middle names?"

"No."

Ian wrote as fast as he could while trying to keep it legible and fight off the cramp in his right hand. With all the standard clauses it still took twenty minutes and he could see John was tiring.

"I'll just go and get a second witness."

Unfortunately, he could not ask Beth because it was against hospital protocol for staff to witness Wills but luckily, Ian found a visitor in the waiting room that was willing to help.

Ian gave John the whole pad to rest on and passed him

his Montegrappa fountain pen.

John wrapped his fist around it as though it was a dagger and stabbed it into the paper breaking off the tip of the nib. Ian's heart sank.

"Will it still write?" Ian asked. "Just have a go."

"It's not very neat," John said, looking at his scratchy signature.

"That's fine," Ian said, checking the signature could be deciphered. "It's not a calligraphy competition."

Ian and the visitor then signed as witnesses using the visitor's biro.

"That's it. We're done," Ian said. "I hope all goes well this afternoon."

They said their good-byes. Ian walked back to his car lost in his own thoughts when he heard a voice behind him.

"Nice car." He turned around and saw Beth, who must have just finished her shift as she had changed out of her uniform.

"Thank you. She's a bit long in the tooth but I think she's a classic."

"Like her owner," Beth said, and then rather embarrassedly, "classic, I mean, not long in the tooth."

Ian laughed. "That's okay, you're probably right on both counts. I say, you don't fancy a coffee, do you? I could do with a break after that little episode."

"No, thanks. I've just finished a twelve-hour shift and

I'm off to bed," she hesitated and then said, "but I could meet you for a drink tonight if you like?"

Ian was a bit taken aback by her forwardness but reacted positively.

"Excellent. Where do you fancy? How about The Squinting Cat?" He said referring to a country-style pub a couple of miles outside Harrogate.

"The Squinting Cat is fine. Shall we say about 8.00 PM?"

"Perfect. Do you want me to pick you up?"

"No. I'll see you there."

Ian lowered himself into the E-type and headed back to the office. So, she thinks I'm classic, does she? He mused. Maybe it was his navy-blue suit from Anderson & Sheppard in Savile Row or perhaps she noticed the tailored shirt from Turnbull & Asser. He was fantasising now.

The simple truth was that, although Beth would normally date a more rough and ready type, she recognised a good-looking man when she saw one and she hoped that a relationship with a young professional might produce a better outcome than her more recent experiences.

Ian arrived at The Squinting Cat just before 8.00 PM and was surprised to see Beth already seated at the bar. He checked his watch which was a Rolex Explorer in case he was late, but he was bang on time.

Beth gave him a nice smile and Ian thought she

looked pretty in her maroon, silky camisole top which she was wearing with skinny jeans and black leather boots. "What would you like to drink?" She asked.

Ian was taken off guard. He came from a background where the man always paid but she was there before him and obviously had just bought herself a drink.

"I'm terribly sorry. I should have got this."

Beth smiled again. "Don't worry. You can get the next one. Now, what would you like?"

"I'll have a pint of Tetley's please," Ian said, still feeling awkward.

They moved to a small table beside a glowing log fire.

"I've never had to do a death bed Will before," Ian said to start the conversation. "I was given the impression John Field was about to die but I hope he's going to be okay?"

Beth's response was matter of fact.

"He's had a serious operation, but it should give him a couple of more years so long as he doesn't get an infection. That fall this morning, though, was the last thing he needed."

The time was passing quickly as they searched in their conversation for areas of common interest when Beth glanced through the double-sided bar into a separate section of the pub.

"Oh, there's Fraser," she said. "He was my fiancé."

Not for the first time that evening, Ian looked embarrassed.

"Do you want to go over and see him?"

"Oh, no. I broke it off with him. The wedding invitations had gone out and everything, but I got cold feet. I just wasn't ready to get married. I'm only twenty-two."

Ian did wonder if he was there for Fraser's benefit, but he managed to salvage the conversation and they enjoyed the rest of the evening. When it got to about 10.30 PM, Ian felt he should bring things to a close.

"Well, we'd better get back. Do you want a lift home, or did you drive?"

"Yes please, to the lift home and no I didn't drive. Some friends brought me."

Beth lived near the hospital in a house converted into four flats. Ian pulled up outside and pushed himself out of the Jag so he could open the car door for her.

With Ian's father having died before girls were on Ian's horizon, he had only ever received one piece of advice from his mother in relation to dating. 'Never ask if you can kiss her. Just do it. She will let you know if it's welcome or not.'

Taking this on-board Ian leaned in towards Beth to kiss her goodnight. He intended to give her just a brief kiss on the lips, but her mouth opened, and they fell into a long and passionate kiss. Time seemed to vanish but eventually, they parted. Beth looked up into his eyes.

"Do you want to come upstairs?" Just sex. It mustn't

mean anything."

Her words were like a stab to his heart. How could she say, 'it mustn't mean anything?'

"Sorry, I've an early start tomorrow. I'd better get back."

"Oh, no. I hope I haven't upset you. It's just that my friends say I don't need a relationship, I just need to get back out there and have some fun."

"No, it's fine," Ian said, trying to cover up his feelings. "I just need to get back. I'll call you."

Ian had been a little subdued over the following two weeks. He hadn't contacted Beth, but he had been out for a game of squash with his best friend Rupert and told him all about Beth over a couple of pints afterwards. Rupert had been quite indignant on Ian's behalf.

"You absolutely did the right thing," he reassured him. "You're more than a rebound."

Ian was feeling a little thick-headed when he walked into the office at just past nine the following morning. He was barely through the door before Sarah, the rather feisty receptionist shouted at him.

"Ian, Mr Field's been on the phone. He wants a new Will and he needs a home visit."

Chapter Three

April 1987 – North Yorkshire

Helperby was not the easiest of places to get to but Ian enjoyed home visits and he was looking forward to the drive so he could put the E-type through its paces.

The roads were damp as it had been raining and he realised they would be greasy, but he still chose the most direct route avoiding the A1. It was about sixteen miles from Harrogate, and he allowed thirty minutes to complete the journey.

The country roads were twisty, and he threw the car into the corners just keeping it at its road holding limit. The stiff chassis and supple suspension gave it great traction, but no car is infallible and as the back wheels started to slip, he would apply a little opposite lock to bring it back under control.

"This is more like dancing than driving," he said to himself as he skirted around another corner.

Riverside House was up a private track overlooking Helperby Common and the River Swale. It was modern; one of four. The first three faced the track and then

Riverside House stood at the end, set at right angles to the other three, its front looking down the track and its rear view being of the Common and the river.

If you ignored the garages, you could say it was a standard three-bedroomed detached house with its front gable end facing the track with a front door up some steps. If you faced the door, to the right-hand side was the sitting room window and then above the door and the sitting room, the bedroom windows. But that would be to ignore the rather spectacular feature of this property. On the left-hand side was a large garage over which, the roofline of the house had been extended from its centre ridge. Above the garage was a room, shaped like a wedge of cheese, with normal ceiling heights on the right-hand side but tapering to just a few feet on the left. It had two picture windows at the back and front, which made the most of the views.

Ian jogged up the steps and knocked loudly on the door.

"Come in, come in," John Field shouted.

Ian let himself in and headed for the sitting room from where the voice had emanated.

John was seated in an office chair at a mahogany bureau with a breathing mask over his face and an oxygen cylinder beside him. Ian gave him a broad smile and John quickly pulled off the mask. Ian walked over to him and shook his hand.

"How are you?"

"Well, I'm still alive! Forgive me if I don't get up. I get out of breath very quickly and my wound is now infected."

"I'm sorry to hear that," Ian said, pulling a face to indicate disappointment. "I understand you would like to change your Will?"

"Yes. I've reconciled with my wife, Diane."

"Oh, that's good," Ian replied, wondering if John's state of health had been an influencing factor in her decision.

"Well, I need someone to look after me. You would have met her, but she's gone shopping. Anyway, I want to leave her the income from my Estate during her lifetime. Then after her death, I want the capital to pass to the children. And I want you to be an Executor, to see fair play because she and the children don't get on."

"Can you give me an idea of what the Estate consists of?" Ian asked.

"Well, this house."

"Which will pass to Diane anyway as it's outside the Estate." Ian reminded him.

"Yes, I understand. And I have six terraced houses in Ripon. My grandfather bought one side of the street from the builder in the early 1900s."

"Are they the ones on Victoria Avenue? I think I've seen the deeds in the strong-room."

"Yes, they're the ones. All let, and the rents will

be enough for Diane to live on. And she will have her pension, of course."

"Have you any savings?"

"I have about £100,000 in The Building Society."

"What about shares?"

"No."

"Have you any valuable furniture or personal items?"

There was a short silence before John answered.

"I thought we might come to that. Do you know what a Luger looks like?"

"The gun?" Ian asked, somewhat surprised.

"Yes."

"Well, I had a toy one as a boy."

John paused, opened one of the small drawers in the bureau and pulled out some keys. He passed them to Ian.

"There's a room up those stairs on the left. I keep it locked and don't allow anyone else in. If you go in, you will see some guns I've laid out on a table. I've just cleaned them. Bring the Luger back down with you and next to it you will see a watch and a wallet. Bring those as well."

Ian went upstairs as instructed and opened the door. The light flooded in from the two picture windows, but Ian's eyes went straight to a table in the centre of the room. Lying across either side of the table was a shotgun and a stalking rifle. In between, he could see a variety of handguns, some oily rags and a tin of oil. To the right of these lay the Luger, watch and wallet. He picked them up, returned downstairs and handed them over to John.

John passed the Luger back to him.

"Handle it," he said. "Tell me what it feels like. It's not loaded."

Ian held the Luger in his right hand and kept turning it over from side to side. He put his finger through the trigger ring and pointed it towards the window. It fitted into his hand perfectly. He felt the weight of it and the smoothness of the metal, which was cold.

"It's beautiful," he said, "superbly balanced. It just comes to hand."

"Doesn't it!" John exclaimed. "And yet it's lethal."

Ian didn't say anything. He was still looking at the gun and thinking.

"I took it off an SS officer I shot during the War. Captain Manfred Fuchs was his name. That's his watch and wallet." John said, pointing at the items he had placed on the bureau.

Ian was trying to take it all in.

"I haven't killed anything since. Not even a fly."

"My father was in the War," Ian said. "He was an Eighth Army Desert Rat, but he never really talked about it and by the time I wanted to ask him he had died."

"What Regiment was he in?"

"The Royal Signals, although I appreciate it's a Corps, not a Regiment."

Ian put the gun down.

"The problem is none of the handguns are licensed and that probably makes my possession of them illegal. I don't want to call the police because they might charge me. I'd rather leave them to you in my Will and you can sort it out. After I'm dead, there is nothing they can do."

"There's no need to mention them in the Will. If we say nothing, they will form part of the Residuary Estate. I can then inform the police and they will send a firearms officer to take them away. The shotgun and stalking rifle we should be able to sell to a licensed dealer who can collect them from the police, but I don't know about the handguns. Perhaps they can be sold to a collector."

"That's fine," John said, somewhat relieved. "You've already got it all worked out! Now have a look at the watch."

Ian picked up the watch and looked at it.

"This is a rather nice Rolex. It could be valuable."

"Yes, that's what I thought, and I see you're wearing a Rolex so you must know something about them."

Ian glanced down at his watch. It was a Rolex Explorer. Larger than Fuchs's model, it was steel with a black dial and a black leather strap. The positions for three, six and nine o'clock were marked in Arabic numerals and there was an inverted triangle in the twelve o'clock position. Ian liked its simplicity and it was one of his most prized possessions.

"It was my father's. This model was designed in 1953 following the ascent of Everest by Sir Edmund Hillary and Tenzing Norgay. It's funny because everyone thinks about Rolexes as being waterproof but my father had admired them ever since the Second World War because after years in the desert he said he had noticed that they were the only watches that could keep out the sand."

"He was right about that. The sand got everywhere. That's why looking after your kit could make the difference between life and death."

"Were you a Desert Rat?" Ian's voice suddenly rose in excitement.

"No, a Royal Marine but we got about."

"Oh, I trained with the Royal Marines," Ian was getting animated. "I was in the CCF at school and the Royal Marines came and gave us a talk. At the end of the talk, the Officer said he had asked three of his men to hide in our shrubbery and we all ran out to try and find them. We found one buried in the compost heap and another lying in camouflaged netting suspended from a tree, but we couldn't find the third."

"There were probably only two!" John intervened.

"Anyway, everyone in the CCF had to go on one week's summer camp and because I was in the naval section, I got chosen to spend a week with the Royal Marines in Scotland."

"Which school did you go to?"

"Sedbergh," Ian replied and to anyone in the know, especially Yorkshiremen, that one word said it all. Sedbergh was an all-boys boarding school set in an isolated position in the Yorkshire Dales. It was renowned for its toughness and the famous Wilson Run which comprised a ten-mile race over the fells. Every pupil had to complete the course, even if they were not in the race, annually in March and if their performance wasn't good enough, they got sent around again.

"Ah, that explains it. You look more like a Marine than a lawyer!" John said teasingly.

Ian was tall and athletic. He had run the 800 meters at County level and represented the school for two seasons during which time he was unbeaten although this had more to do with his mental strength rather than any physical advantages. He was determined and indomitable.

"I wanted to do a short-term commission in the Marines, but with it taking six years to qualify as a solicitor, it all just seemed too long. I was desperate for a green beret though."

"It commands a heavy price," he sighed. "Now, let's get back to the watch."

"Yes, sorry," Ian said, feeling a bit like a silly schoolgirl.

"Have you read the inscription on the back?"

Ian had seen it but hadn't really taken it in, so he had another look and chewed over the words, 'To my Freddie, always yours, Judith.'

"Does anything strike you as odd?" John pressed him.

"Well," said Ian, thinking as he was speaking, "I wonder why the inscription is in English and I'm not sure if Freddie is the correct shortening for Manfred."

"Exactly, what I thought."

Ian looked at the wallet.

"Can I open it?"

"Be my guest."

It was a well-worn, brown leather, bifold wallet. When Ian opened it, he immediately saw the picture of the woman and child behind a cellophane picture pocket. He made the obvious comment.

"I wonder if this is Judith?"

"That would be a reasonable assumption," John replied.

Ian pulled out the identity card. There was a photograph of Manfred Fuchs, partially covered by an Eagle stamp. There was a number and his name. Ian noticed his date of birth – the 22nd April 1914. There was a name for next of kin and an address – Rubens Strasse 18, Munich.

The story was becoming all too real. There was a man with a family. Ian was touching his possessions and he was sitting with the man who had killed him.

"I want to leave you the watch and wallet in my Will and I would like you to go to Germany, try to trace his family and give them back."

Ian thought for a moment and being a lawyer, his first

thoughts were of the legal aspects.

"Again, I don't think we need anything in the Will," Ian said. "There has been a transfer of possession of the watch and wallet to you, but not a transfer of ownership. They still belong to the heirs of Manfred Fuchs so in that respect, to return them would be the right thing to do but I'm not sure if this is something I want to get involved with."

"I'll give you money to cover your expenses."

"It's not a matter of money. I just don't think I have the time."

John could see the hesitation on Ian's face.

"I don't regret killing Fuchs," John said. "The SS were bastards. God only knows what he did in his lifetime or what he would have gone on to do if I hadn't killed him. But I do regret taking his watch and wallet, especially given the inscription and the photograph. It has all just become a little too personal and returning them would bring some sort of closure."

"Let me think about it," Ian said as he stood up to leave. "I will have this Will typed up and come back in a few days to get it signed. I will have to bring two witnesses with me because if I'm going to be an Executor, I cannot witness the Will."

"That's fine." John pushed himself up by leaning on the bureau, which creaked precariously, and with difficulty, walked Ian to the door. Seeing the blue E-type parked on the drive, he remarked on how stylish it looked. "What a beautiful car. You don't see many like that nowadays."

"Another gift from my father," Ian replied.

Ian lowered himself into the Jag and looked back at John, who was standing in the doorway. He noticed how one side of his chest had a sunken look. It was as though the left-hand side of his torso was collapsing, which was not surprising given that his lung had been removed.

The Jag was just pulling away when John signalled Ian to stop. He edged down the steps and resting his hand on the soft top vinyl hood, he lent into the driver's side window which Ian had opened.

"Do think about my offer," John said. "It's just something didn't feel right about this one. I don't know if it was the dodgy Belgian intelligence, the reminder about targeting the officers and bringing back the dog tags or the fact that the Commanding Officer seemed to recognise the name, but something stinks. To me, it felt more like an assassination."

Chapter Four

April 1987 – North Yorkshire

The Head of HR was being awkward. Ian wanted to take two secretaries with him to get the Will signed but Gavin Cox was resisting.

"Why can't he come into the office?" Was his suggestion.

"Because he is dying and is attached to an oxygen cylinder," Ian replied rather bluntly. He didn't like being challenged.

"Why can't you get a neighbour to witness the Will?" Cox persisted.

"Because we need two witnesses and the Will is highly personal and confidential." Ian wasn't giving up.

"Look Sutherland you might fancy a light Wednesday afternoon gallivanting off with a couple of secretaries, but we can't let them have that much time out of the office."

Cox had revealed his true feelings now and it was clear they didn't like each other. Cox was a jobs-worth box-ticking parasite, in Ian's opinion and as far as Cox was concerned, Sutherland was a cavalier risk-taker, complying with the rules only when he thought it was necessary.

Ian narrowed his eyes and lowered his tone, speaking quietly but with authority.

"I am being made an Executor of a Trust from which this firm is likely to make substantial fees for several decades. I am charging for the Will at an hourly rate and to bring these matters to a conclusion I need to take two witnesses with me to the home of the client. If you really have a problem with this, speak with Hannah. If the senior partner doesn't stop me in the next half hour, I'm going."

Hannah was the third generation of Ryders to take the helm at the family firm and the first woman to be senior partner. She was a well-respected family lawyer but had no experience of management, so when it became her turn to take charge, she was susceptible to siren voices. However, Ian knew Hannah had a soft spot for him and wouldn't object so he went straight up to the secretaries' office on the top floor and walked over to two of his favourites, Julie and Debbie.

People joked that Julie and Debbie must be twins as they did everything together. They were both tall blondes. Both married, aged about thirty-five and both had two young children. Also, they both had to contend with the drudgery of coping with domesticity while being married to men on low incomes, who wanted their dinner on the table at six o'clock and seemed to show little appreciation of the fact that they were married to highly attractive women. Ian knew, therefore, that as a younger non-predatory male with a broad smile, he was on to a winner.

"Good morning, ladies. I was wondering if you would like a little trip out to Helperby to witness a Will? One of you will need to drive but you will get expenses and we could stop off for a coffee on the way back?"

Both girls looked at each other with a sort of 'can we' expression.

"Is it all right with Gavin Cox?" Debbie asked, looking concerned.

"Yes, no problem," Ian replied. "Hannah's okay with it."

Looking at each other for approval, they both smiled and nodded and made some affirmative noises.

"Great," Ian said. "We'll go at about 2.00 PM."

With Debbie driving in her old VW Golf they took the slightly longer A1 route but still got there in good time for the 3.00 PM appointment.

Mrs Field answered the door. She was trim, medium height and had short, curly, brown hair, thanks to the skills of the hairdresser. She had no distinguishing features, although she looked at Ian suspiciously in a 'what have you and my husband cooked up between you' sort of way.

After the usual introductions, she took the three of them through to her husband who was sitting at his bureau, offered drinks which were declined, then disappeared into the kitchen.

Julie, the slightly more attractive of the two ladies, walked in first and John immediately stood up, smiling. Ian saw him take in the above the knee black skirt and court shoes, the white blouse and long blonde hair. She was swiftly followed by a similar if somewhat more apprehensive version in the equally acceptable form of Debbie.

Ian noticed that John looked more drawn than last time he visited and slightly feverish but there was no way John was going to let the ladies realise this. Before Ian could make any introductions, John took over.

"Well, you have surpassed yourself Ian, bringing such attractive visitors to my home. I'm John Field, how do you do?"

"Hello, I'm Julie."

"And I'm Debbie."

"Do sit down. Would you like a drink?"

"No, thank you. We've just been offered one," Julie replied.

"Good. Well, let's not worry about the Will. You tell me all about yourselves."

Ian let the game playing continue while Julie and Debbie answered questions about their children and John regaled them with stories about his sporting prowess before the War. When everyone was settled, he pulled the engrossed Will out of the file.

"Right, back to work, I'm afraid," Ian said when John paused for breath.

"To recap this Will appoints your two children, Edward and Janet, as executors along with myself. It leaves everything to your wife, Diane, for her lifetime and after her death, the estate will be divided equally between Edward and Janet. I have also added a clause about grandchildren. God forbid Edward or Janet should predecease you, but if either of them did, that person's children would take their parents share equally between them. So, if Edward had two children and he predeceased you his children would get one-quarter of the estate each on Diane's death. Does that all make sense?"

"I think so," John replied a little bored, "but it's very unlikely given my current state of health. Anyway, Edward has just one daughter, Lucy. Janet hasn't got any children. She married badly and divorced quite quickly."

"Okay, so in that situation, if anything happened to Edward, Lucy would inherit his share and if anything happened to Janet, it would all go to Edward," Ian explained.

"That's fine," John said, "and this house will be Diane's outright, won't it?"

"Yes. The house will pass by what we call survivorship so it will not form part of your estate. It will belong to Diane free of any trust and she will be able to do what she likes with it."

"Well, I think that's only right," John said. "After all, she has put up with me all these years. Don't you agree, ladies?"

Julie and Debbie nodded.

"Have you any other questions?" Ian asked.

John shook his head.

"Right, let's get it signed," Ian said, reaching for what looked like a fountain pen lying on John's desk.

"That won't do you any good," John said, laughing, "not for this job anyway."

Ian looked at him, enquiringly.

"Open it."

It looked like an ordinary fountain pen just short of six inches long. Ian unscrewed the cap to reveal a four-inch stiletto blade. The cap formed the handle into which the blade was embedded; the rest of the pen was the cover for the blade.

Ian looked at it in surprise.

"It's a spy pen."

"Wow," Ian said, playing with it. "That's interesting."

"Well, you can have it if you like it," John said nonchalantly.

"Oh, I couldn't," Ian said. "It wouldn't be right."

"Look, I want you to have it. I broke your pen, remember? Think of this as a replacement. I would like you to have it as a memento of our friendship."

Ian looked a little embarrassed, but Julie and Debbie

indicated their approval

"Well, when you put it like that - thank you," he said, putting the pen in his jacket pocket.

John and then Julie and Debbie signed the Will and then Ian asked Debbie to date it. She wrote 22nd April 1987. Ian suddenly realised it was the birthday of Manfred Fuchs. He would have been 73. Instead, he had been shot aged 30. John was 71. His own father had died aged 61. These thoughts were swimming around his head, and he went silent. John noticed and picked up the conversation.

"I may want to change my Will if it means you will bring Julie and Debbie back to see me," John said, rising from his chair. They all laughed.

John walked them to the front door and as Ian stood back to allow Julie and Debbie out first, John put his arm around Ian's shoulder and held him back. Julie and Debbie walked to the car and John whispered in Ian's ear.

"Have you given any more thought to my request?"

Ian hadn't but impulsively, without understanding his own reasoning, he agreed.

"Yes," Ian said. "I will go to Munich, try to find Fuchs's relatives and return the watch and wallet to them."

John's face relaxed.

"Thank you," he said his arm still around Ian's shoulder.

Ian broke away and held out his hand.

"I hope I see you again soon."

"Yes, that would be nice. I'm struggling to shake off this infection, but as soon as I have, I'll be fine."

Ian jumped in the Golf and he and the girls waved good-bye. John watched them drive away, went inside and collapsed onto his bed. He had made a supreme effort to put on a good show but after the strain of the meeting, he was exhausted.

Ian, Julie and Debbie went straight back to the office as there wasn't really time for coffee. The girls had enjoyed their trip out but wanted to tidy their desks and get home so Ian logged the Will into the strong room and went home too.

Ian lived in a rented flat overlooking Valley Gardens in Harrogate. It was nothing special and simply comprised an open plan living room and kitchen and one bedroom with an en suite bathroom. To be honest, Ian found living on his own lonely, so he liked to keep busy and decided to go on a run.

He could have run around the Valley Gardens and through the nearby pinewoods and sometimes he did, but he needed some space to clear his mind, so he decided to do his favourite run near Fountains Abbey.

Ian changed into his running kit and drove to the village of Studley Roger, parking on Studley Lane near Lawrence House. He then set off slowly up Plumpton Lane but rather than bearing right into Studley Park he continued straight uphill through Mackershaw Wood, the incline increasing steadily until he reached the southern boundary of the deer park.

Ian was gasping for breath and sweating by the time he reached the kissing gate into the park but he was used to the steep hills around Sedbergh and as the gradient had increased Ian had simply slowed his pace, stood tall and breathed deeply.

He paused for a second as he weaved through the gate and surveyed the view before him. This was his favourite part of the run – about one mile, all gently downhill, across the broad open landscape of the deer park.

Lengthening his stride and running with a spring in his step he, subconsciously, processed his promise to John Field. He felt a desire to discover the truth. What that was, he did not know but he became a lawyer because he had a strong sense of justice and fair play. John felt there was more to Manfred's death than met the eye and instinctively, Ian felt it too.

He had committed himself to go to Munich and his promise went beyond the normal bounds of client service, but he was, at least, able to console himself with the thought that he would not have to fulfil his obligations anytime soon.

John didn't get up on Thursday morning. He was quite simply exhausted and feverish. Diane attended to his immediate needs, but he couldn't eat anything. On Friday, he was worse, and Diane called the doctor. John had insisted on staying at home so the doctor did what she could to make him comfortable, including administering some morphine.

On Saturday, John was clearly deteriorating. He was drifting in and out of sleep and hallucinating. The district nurse attended in the morning and gave Diane a special number to call in an emergency, saying a doctor would come to the house.

On Sunday morning, the crisis arrived, and the fever peaked. John was burning up but was soaking wet with sweat and when not sweating, he was shivering. He simply couldn't breathe. The lack of breath made him panic, cough and gasp for air. His one remaining lung was gulping for it in a last desperate attempt to make up the deficit. Diane was out of her depth and called the doctor, who said this was the end. She injected some morphine and John sank back into the pillows, more relaxed but breathing only shallowly. His eyes closed. He saw his parents. He saw a Dalmatian he had as a child. He saw his rifle and Manfred Fuchs collapsing. He saw Ian. Then he exhaled. Not the steadying exhale of a sniper but the final expulsion of the air from the body as the soul passed away. John Field was dead.

Chapter Five

April 1987 – North Yorkshire

The call from Diane Field came soon after 9.00 AM on
Monday morning. Ian knew it would come one day but
he was not expecting it so soon. There was the shocked
silence; the embarrassing struggle for the appropriate
words of consolation and then the legal response setting
out the necessary formalities.

Ian said the usual protocol would be to have the
funeral first and then, perhaps the next day, a meeting
with the executors and residuary beneficiaries. However,
in this case, there was the complication of the guns. Ian
tentatively broached the subject with Diane.

"I'm afraid some of them are unlicensed. We really
should ask the police to come and secure them straight
away."

"That's fine by me," Diane said. "I hate the things. I
don't want anything to do with them. Will you arrange
it?"

"I can do. Will you be in all day?"

"Yes, but the undertaker is coming at 11.00 AM so

leave it until this afternoon. You will be here to hand them over, won't you? I don't want to touch them."

"Yes, I'll be there and when the police have gone, you can brief me about the funeral arrangements," Ian replied.

Ian rang North Yorkshire police headquarters and a telephone operator said a firearms officer would meet Ian on site at 2.00 PM. This would mean leaving the office just after 1.00 PM so, around midday, Ian nipped into town to grab a sandwich. It was then it started sinking in and Ian relived the death of his own father.

He was walking along the pavement but having an out of body experience. It was as though he was looking down and could see himself walking along. He was on a path with grass either side of it and he could see the route before him. He kept walking, an empty body, embarking on an unwanted journey, not knowing where he was going.

Ian had liked John and John had liked Ian. They had made a connection, but he did not know why. Something linked them and Ian could only think that in each other they saw a little bit of themselves.

Now John was dead, and Ian had a job to do. He would do what was right regardless of hindrance. He would fulfil his duties as executor and keep his promise to his friend. Another person lost, like his father, taken away from him at all too early an age. That had broken his heart and he had screamed to the heavens, 'Why?' Only years later did he appreciate, 'for everything its season,' but the wound ran deep.

Ian came back down to earth on his arrival at M&S, where a homeless man sat outside the entrance. Ian glanced at the hat on the floor containing a few coins but walked past, without giving eye contact, knowing that any money he gave would be spent on the wrong things. He went inside, bought two packets of prawn sandwiches, and left the way he came, dropping one packet in the hat as he quickly walked past the homeless man. The homeless man looked up to thank him, but Ian simply nodded and walked on.

Ian had only been at Riverside House a few minutes when a police van pulled up on the drive. Ian went out to introduce himself. PC Chris Williamson was surprisingly friendly and quite relaxed about the situation.

"We get a lot of these," he said. "It's amazing how many soldiers brought home trophies from the War."

Ian handed over the entire cache and said he would contact Bonhams auctioneers, who had a specialist gun department, regarding a possible sale.

The PC was completely amenable. "We just want to prevent these weapons from getting into the wrong hands. That's why we often declare an amnesty so people can hand them in."

"Well that went better than I expected," Ian said as he joined Mrs Field who was in the back garden cutting some flowers.

"How did the meeting with the undertaker go?"

"Fine but the funeral can't be until the 8th of May as the crematorium in Harrogate is very busy. I'm not going to bother with a church service. We can go straight to the crematorium and then I will book a funeral tea at The Ripon Spa Hotel afterwards as Ripon is where the family comes from. I will then have his ashes interred in the cemetery privately."

"I will attend the funeral if you don't mind," Ian said.

"Oh, of course, you must, and I hope you will come back to the Spa afterwards. That way, you can meet Edward and Janet and answer any questions they may have."

Diane must have thought this was a good introduction to the subject because she then quizzed Ian about the Will. He reassured her that the house was hers and she would receive the rental income from the tenanted properties and other investments after expenses. She didn't like the fact that she wasn't an executrix, but she seemed content enough, knowing that Ian would see fair play. If she gave anything away, it was a sense of relief that John hadn't done something more drastic given their rather strained relationship.

Ian arrived at Stonefall cemetery on this dull and damp afternoon a good twenty minutes before the appointed time and as the previous funeral was just finishing. It was like a conveyor belt with one funeral after another.

Mourners queued for their turn. The presiding Minister knew only the basics about the deceased and there was little time for any true depth of feeling or paying proper homage to the life that had been led.

If you weren't a church member with a church family, your despatch into the next world would be very impersonal, Ian thought.

Ian took a seat at the back of the chapel as soon as he could and then watched the attendees file in. They were mostly elderly with a few Army types and a couple of ladies probably in their sixties. Ian wondered if they were old flames given that John had been a bit of a ladies' man.

Ian noticed a tall, distinguished-looking gentleman, probably in his seventies. His frame was slightly bent now but he had a well-defined nose and some of the other men seemed to acknowledge him in a deferential sort of way.

Finally, the family came in and it was fairly obvious who they were. Ted Field looked a bit like his father but slimmer and he had a moustache, very much the RAF officer. A lady held on to his left arm, presumably his wife and he held the hand a young girl.

That must be Lucy, Ian thought, and given her clear upset and youthfulness, it was probably her first funeral.

Another lady walked beside them, and Ian guessed this was Janet. Diane followed just behind, accompanied to her seat by the funeral director who had recognised that she was on her own.

The Service followed the usual format; a reading from John 14, Psalm 23 sung as a hymn and prayers for the family. There was a brief eulogy from the Minister with information gleaned from Diane which he read carefully, especially checking his notes when mentioning names of the family. On the way out, there was a collection for Cancer Research and a clammy handshake from the Minister offering his condolences even though he had no idea of the relationship between the deceased and the person before him.

It was with relief, therefore, that Ian entered The Spa Hotel where he was ushered into a sun lounge with picture windows overlooking the manicured lawns and flower beds of the award-winning gardens.

Ian accepted a soft drink and walked over to the distinguished-looking gentleman with the aquiline nose.

"Hello, I'm Ian Sutherland," Ian said, holding out his hand. "I'm the family lawyer."

Lieutenant Colonel Alan Skinner grabbed Ian's hand and held on to it for what seemed like an inordinate amount of time. He looked Ian in the eye with a piercing glare that was slightly unnerving. Ian was clearly being weighed up.

"And I'm Alan Skinner; retired officer. I used to keep a fatherly eye on these old reprobates when they retired," he said gesturing towards some of the ex-army personnel chatting in the sun lounge.

"Did you know John well?"

"We spent a bit of time together towards the end of the War; Battle of the Bulge and all that but I haven't seen him for years."

Not many people would say what Ian said next and Ian realised that as he said it, but he went ahead as this was an opportunity he didn't want to miss.

"Does the name Manfred Fuchs mean anything to you?"

Alan Skinner straightened himself upright and then gave Ian that piercing look again. He linked his arm under Ian's and pulled him towards the French doors.

"Let's have a walk around the garden."

Alan Skinner led Ian through the French doors and down a couple of steps towards the croquet lawn. When they were out of earshot, he continued.

"So, what do you know about Manfred Fuchs?"

"Just that John shot him and took his Luger from the dead body. He also took his wallet and a watch," Ian replied.

"A lot of them did that I'm afraid; spoils of war. What is it to you?"

"Well the watch turns out to be quite valuable and John asked me to try to trace Fuchs's relatives and return it; and the wallet."

"Good luck with that!" Skinner said scathingly.

Ian didn't want to give too much away but he realised

that Skinner was not going to volunteer any information without being pressed.

"It just seems strange, or so John thought years later, that so much interest should be shown in a young Captain even if he had won the iron cross."

"Look, there was a propaganda war going on. There were standing orders to take out the officers first and the military hierarchy wanted to know who they'd got; dead or alive. Granted, Fuchs wasn't a senior figure, but the request came from Colonel Granville and he wanted to know if we came across him."

A sudden recognition dawned on Ian's face.

"Do you mean Lord Granville from Granville's bank?"

"That's the one," Skinner replied. "He's a nasty old bugger and for some reason he wanted us to let him know if we got Fuchs so when Field killed him, I sent Granville the dog tag. In fact, if I remember correctly, it was Granville who suggested we sent in snipers."

This was just getting interesting when they were interrupted by Ted Field.

"Hello, I'm Ted; any chance of a quick word with you?" He said, looking at Ian.

Alan Skinner grabbed his chance to escape.

"I'll leave you two in peace. Nice talking to you, Mr Sutherland."

Ted asked a few brief questions about the Will which Ian answered and it was agreed that Ted, Janet and Diane would come into the office the following day for a more formal explanation.

Ted was an agreeable chap and Ian asked him to bring the wallet and watch with him having told him where they were and the story behind them. There was no resistance on the part of Ted although Ian was careful to slip in the fact that the items were not legally part of his father's estate.

Ian said his good-byes and then slipped away in the E-type back to his flat in Valley Drive.

Ian knew a little of Lord Granville. He had been Chairman and now in his early nineties, was Life President of Granville's bank which was a private bank for the well-to-do. He had an estate about ten miles North East of Harrogate and a few years ago Ian had attended a dinner with his friend Duncan Jones where Lord Granville was the guest speaker. When he stood up to speak, Granville was already well-oiled and slurring his words. People found this funny to start with and he did tell an amusing anecdote. He spoke about the importance of winning and illustrated this with a story about his schooldays at Harrow. When he was in the third form, he had played cricket for the school in an away match against Eton and Eton had beaten Harrow easily. When they got back to school, the entire team was given six strokes of the cane by the Headmaster for lack of effort 'including the scorer!'

Ian would never forget the way the room erupted with

laughter when Lord Granville said, "including the scorer."

However, the speech then got a little darker. Granville talked about his blue blood. His family had come to England in the twelfth century and although he could be rightly proud of his lineage, Granville genuinely believed this made him a superior human being. He went on about this at such length that diners got up to leave preferring their own company in the bar.

Within half an hour, Ian reached the Valley Gardens and pulled up in the first available parking place. Although late in the afternoon, the sun was breaking through the clouds and the gardens glistened in the gentle light.

Well, fancy that, Ian thought to himself. Lord Granville. What a small world! He was an unpleasant man. In fact, if you didn't know better, you'd think he was a Nazi.

Chapter Six

August 1987 – London

Sinking into the back seat of the taxi at Kings Cross Ian started to relax.

"The Ritz please," Ian said, and the taxi driver nodded and pulled away slowly into the London traffic.

London was one of Ian's favourite places in the world and The Ritz was one of his favourite places in London.

As the taxi weaved a route through the cars, buses and delivery vans that congested the Capital Ian wondered what it was that made London so special? He loved the atmosphere of enterprise and the visible deployment of capital. Businesspeople, politicians, lawyers, artisans and ambassadors, all busy as bees endeavouring to achieve. He liked the excitement in the shops and theatres, the glamour of the hotels and restaurants and the history of the museums and monuments; but most of all he liked London simply because he could be himself.

Ian had inherited some money when his father died. Not a fortune but the income was enough to keep him in decent suits and give him independence and a lifestyle in tune with his education. In London, he could leave behind the petty jealousies of parochial professionals and be his own man. He could stay where he wanted, eat where he wanted and wear what he wanted without someone asking how he could afford it. Ian wasn't ostentatious with his wealth, but he had good taste and purchased accordingly.

The taxi dropped Ian at St. James's Street and he walked through the revolving doors of The Ritz into the foyer with its central table festooned with fresh flowers. Immediately, Michael, a concierge par excellence, came to greet him.

"Welcome home sir."

Ian beamed. How lovely to think of The Ritz as one's London home.

"Thank you, Michael." Ian always made a point of remembering names. "It's good to be back."

Ian turned to the Reception area, where three ladies of various nationalities were on hand to assist. Sabine, who was French, gave Ian a broad smile.

"Welcome to The Ritz Mr Sutherland. Your room is all ready for you, and we've upgraded your reservation to room number 107 overlooking Green Park."

Sabine left the reception and showed Ian to his room personally. It was so much more interesting than the anodyne bedrooms of the large hotel chains with their bland colour schemes and modern prints on the walls. This was a blue themed room with luxurious draped curtains and a silk embroidered bedspread. There was an elegant fireplace with a table and chairs in front of it and historic art on the walls.

There was no way Ronnie Roberts would agree to Ian going to Munich in work time, despite it being John Field's wish that the trip was made. In fact, he had seemed quite irritated by the whole idea. 'A wild goose chase,' he called it, so Ian had decided to take a holiday – hence the delay until August when, owing to school holidays, Ian's workload was light.

Ian was flying from Heathrow so he could do a couple of jobs in London on the way and the first of these was a visit to a second-hand watch dealer whose business was located in Burlington Arcade.

Just across the road from The Ritz, Ian was there within a few minutes of unpacking.

Ian didn't want to wear a watch and carry one, so he had decided to wear Manfred's watch for the duration of the trip. He pulled back his sleeve and showed the dealer, then unbuckling the strap he handed him the watch.

"It's a bit small for your wrist if you don't mind me saying Sir."

"It's not mine," Ian replied. "I'm just wearing it for safety while I get it valued. I'm a solicitor and this watch is part of an estate. How much is it worth?"

The dealer raised an eyebrow and put an eyeglass in place.

"It has a soft patina to the face. Collectors like that. Shows it's genuine and the toffee coloured numerals are attractive. These red numerals inside the main chapter ring are unusual though and that makes it more valuable." He removed the eyeglass and looked up. "Can I take the back off?"

"Please do."

The dealer used a rubber grip and unscrewed the back incredibly easily. He looked through his eyeglass again.

"The movement's clean. All looks original. I would say it is worth about £5,000."

"Thank you," Ian said. "I'm not sure what we are doing with it yet."

"Well, you know where to come if you want to sell it," the dealer replied. "Do you want that valuation in writing; for tax purposes?"

"No, thank you, but I will get back to you if I need any more help."

Ian put the watch back on his wrist and headed for Savile Row.

Regardless of any sentimental value the contents of the wallet might have, the watch had a serious monetary value which belonged to Manfred's heirs and in a way, this justified Ian's trip which made him feel able to dismiss Ronnie Roberts's criticism."

Ian turned right at the top end of Burlington Arcade and was soon at his tailors, Anderson & Sheppard.

"Hello Sir. How can we help you?" John, the Head Cutter, Managing Director and holder of the Royal Warrant, asked, shaking Ian's hand.

"Well, I have a couple of twelve-ounce suits, as you know, but I want something lighter for the summer. I was thinking about light grey?" Ian said with enough hesitation to indicate he was open to suggestions.

"I think we will have just the thing for you, Sir. Have a seat and I will bring some samples over to you." John gestured with an open hand towards the brown leather sofa in the centre of the room and Ian sat down.

"Now if you don't mind me saying Sir, you have a fair complexion and this Prince of Wales check will drain the colour from your face." John approached Ian with a large role of light grey cloth which was specially made for Anderson & Sheppard.

"If you would like to stand up Sir, in front of the mirror, I will show you this and then something else for comparison."

Ian stood up and John draped the cloth generously over Ian's shoulders.

"Oh, I see what you mean," Ian said. "It makes me look older."

"I think blue is your colour, Sir. Let me show you this one."

John brought over another role of cloth. It was navy blue and from a distance would look plain, but it actually had the faintest check created with a slightly lighter blue thread woven into the pattern.

"This is a nine-ounce cloth, Sir, made for us by H. Lesser so it is just as light as the grey in weight but more your colouring."

Again, John draped the cloth around Ian's shoulders. It looked so much better with Ian's golden-brown hair and blue eyes.

"Yes," Ian said. "This is much more me."

"Excellent. Well, if you would like to take a seat in the fitting room, I will ask Finn and Danny to be with you shortly."

John drew back a heavy velvet curtain and Ian entered the fitting room which had floor to ceiling mirrors to three sides and a padded leather bench to sit on positioned to one side of the room.

Finn entered first. He was the trouser cutter, and, in some ways, Ian thought he had the harder job because the trousers had to look good but at the same time be comfortable and allow freedom of movement.

"Hello, Sir. How are you?"

"I'm well, thank you Finn. How are you?"

"Oh, I can't complain, Sir. What are we doing, the usual?"

"Yes, please. I'm having a suit made from this lightweight cloth," Ian said pointing to the role of cloth which John had placed on the bench.

"Very good, Sir," Finn said, eying Ian up carefully in his current trousers which he had made a couple of years previously. "You don't seem to have changed shape at all so I will make these up to your existing measurements and then we can make any adjustments at the first fitting."

"That sounds fine, thank you Finn."

"Right Sir, I will send Danny up to see you."

Danny was a younger man than Finn and a Londoner whereas Finn, as his name implied was Irish. Finn did everything by eye and was renowned for being able to cut a pair of trousers to the clients' shape simply by looking at him. Danny, on the other hand, relied more on his tape measure.

Danny shook Ian's hand.

"That's a good choice of cloth, Sir. It will make a lovely suit." Danny said, feeling the cloth. You could see the pride he took in his work.

"Do you want a two-piece or are you having a waistcoat as well?"

Ian thought a three-piece was a bit old fashioned except for the most formal occasions and in any case, this was going to be worn in warmer weather.

"Just a two-piece please," Ian replied.

"Right we are, Sir. Are we sticking with the House style? Single-breasted, three buttons, top button hidden by the lapel?"

"Yes, that's fine."

"Any special requirements?"

"Yes, please." Ian pulled his slim black Ettinger wallet from his inside pocket and handed it to Danny. "Can you make sure the inside pocket on the left-hand side is deep enough for this?"

Danny quickly took a measurement. "Certainly, Sir."

"And I would like a pen pocket on the inside right, narrow enough to prevent my fountain pen from pivoting around."

"Yes, Sir."

Danny took some measurements of Ian's chest and waist and wrote down some figures without commenting.

"When would you like the first fitting, Sir?"

"Well, I'm going to Munich for three days tomorrow," Ian said. "Is there any chance of a fitting when I get back as I'll be in Town?"

"We can do that, Sir. We will look forward to seeing you on Friday."

Ian said his good-byes and then made a dash for Turnbull & Asser on Bury Street where he ordered a couple of bespoke shirts to go with the new suit. He had them made extra-long as he was tall in the body and with extra room around the chest because a slim fit shirt was too tight, but a regular fit had surplus material around his waist.

Returning to The Ritz, Ian wanted to go on a run through Green Park to Hyde Park and then back in a circular route before dinner. The doorman greeted Ian as he approached the steps and then Michael welcomed Ian as he entered the foyer through the revolving doors.

"Can you book a table for me at Scott's tonight please?" Ian asked Michael.

"Certainly, Sir. What time would you like?"

"About 7.30. A table for two."

"I will let you know, Sir."

Ian went to his room, changed into his running kit and set off thinking about the evening to come.

London was humid in August and the traffic rumbled in the background, spewing diesel fumes into the air so that, even though in a park, it wasn't the same as running through Studley Park or Fountains Abbey.

The park was busy with people enjoying all sorts of recreation. Some were running with backpacks, perhaps on their way home and some were running with dogs. Others were just walking or doing exercises, so as Ian entered Hyde Park, he decided to do some sprint training because it was just too distracting to lose oneself in a long-distance run.

Ian found a straight path and paced out 400 meters and then did a series of eight sprints. He split these into pairs of 400, 300, 200 and 100 meters obviously running harder and faster over the shorter distances and resting for a minute at the end of each sprint. This way he built up his speed, peaking at over sixteen mph.

Ian trotted to a stop as he returned to The Ritz and walked up the steps rather red-faced and perspiring. He was a little embarrassed about his appearance but as he entered the foyer, a bellboy was waiting and simply handed him a towel.

"Thank you," Ian said as he quickly pressed the button for the lift.

Ian was meeting Duncan Jones, his friend and investment manager who had taken him to the dinner in Leeds, where the guest speaker had been Lord Granville. Ostensibly, the purpose of the dinner was to discuss his investments, but Ian wanted to see if Duncan could tell him a little more about Lord Granville.

There was a handwritten note from Michael in the bedroom confirming the dinner reservation. Ian picked up the telephone and rang the concierge's number. Michael answered.

"Michael, thank you for confirming Scott's but I forgot to ask you. Can I have a table in the Rivoli Bar for cocktails at about 6.30? I've asked a friend to meet me here and I think he will enjoy the experience."

"Certainly, Sir. I will arrange that for you."

When the phone rang again, it was Michael to say that Duncan had arrived and a table in the cocktail bar awaited them.

Ian bounded into the foyer and gave Duncan a broad smile shaking his hand vigorously.

They were good friends but, in many ways, opposite. Duncan was a little short and carried a few extra pounds. Golf would be the most energetic activity he ever engaged in and that was only in the summer. Duncan was also very cautious. Ian joked that he paid him not for investment ideas but to protect Ian from himself!

Duncan had been an investment manager in Leeds but following the financial deregulation known as Big Bang he had felt he needed the safety of a larger organisation and so he had ended up working for Barclays Wealth Management division. Duncan had kindly moved Ian's portfolio with him, although it wasn't quite large enough to meet Barclays' criteria.

The one thing Ian and Duncan did have in common was a love of investment, so they never lacked conversation and as they sat down at their table in the Rivoli Bar, they were already too deeply animated to pay due attention to the menu.

"I will just have a gin and tonic please," Duncan said to the hovering barman and Ian matched him.

They discussed all the topical subjects, made their way to Scott's ordered the seared scallops and Dover sole with a bottle of Sancerre and then, when the mood of reflection descended, Ian broached what he really wanted to know.

"You know that dinner we went to with Lord Granville?"

"How could I ever forget?" Duncan replied.

"Well, he's just cropped up in relation to one of my estates." Ian then outlined, without mentioning his name, the story of John Field and the Luger and the mysterious involvement of Lord Granville.

"Weren't you thinking of working for Granville's bank at one time?" Ian asked.

"I thought about it but only very briefly," Duncan replied. "The rumour is it has a rather harsh culture."

"I can imagine Lord Granville would not be easy to work for."

"He's out of it now," Duncan said. "The bank is run by his grandson Frederick Granville and he makes his grandfather seem reasonable."

"That bad?" Ian asked, sitting back in his chair.

Duncan looked into his glass and swirled around the last two inches of wine. "Well, he shouts and screams at the staff and thinks the secretaries are his own personal harem."

Ian ordered two espressos which seemed appropriate to their sobering mood and then Duncan walked back to The Ritz with Ian before getting the tube at Green Park. The air was heavy and still, and Ian breathed it in as he watched Duncan disappear down the stairs to the station.

Suddenly, he stopped and came back.

"Look, I wasn't going to mention this as it's only hearsay," Duncan hesitated, "but I understand that one day Frederick's PA didn't turn up for work so a friend went around to see her as she had been out with Frederick the night before. Apparently, she didn't turn up because he'd beaten her senseless."

Duncan gave Ian a concerned look as Ian stared back in disbelief. "All I'm saying is if you're getting involved with the Granvilles, be careful."

Ian meandered back to his room, mulling over Duncan's words. Frederick sounded like a chip off the old block. He inserted his key and unlocked the door shrugging off his fears by amusing himself, murmuring, "It must be genetic."

Chapter Seven

August 1987 – Munich

Ian had a fairly loose plan for his trip to Munich but before he went marching up Rubens Strasse, he wanted to check the electoral roll to see who was living at number 18. It was, after all, over forty years since the end of the war. Secondly, Ian thought he would try to obtain a copy of Manfred's military records just out of interest. If he knew a bit more about Manfred's background, it might be helpful when meeting with the family.

Arriving at Munich airport, Ian was slightly surprised by the weather. It was cloudy with a light breeze just the same as the weather he thought he had left behind in England, and on the drive to the Platzl Hotel, in the centre of town, he noticed that the panorama was flat. He had been expecting to see mountains in the distance!

It was 4.00 PM by the time Ian checked into the Platzl Hotel. He knew nothing about it, but the travel agent had recommended it and it was spotlessly clean with lots of pine furnishings. The receptionists and concierge were not unfriendly, but the atmosphere was a little bit reserved.

Not quite the bonhomie of France or Italy.

Ian hated eating alone but really had no alternative, so he asked the concierge to recommend a restaurant and was advised to turn right outside the hotel and walk around the corner into the main tourist hospitality area.

Immediately, Ian was struck by the impressive white structure of the Hofbrauhaus with its corner bay windows and elegant archways.

It must be worth a look, Ian thought, so he went inside and gazed in amazement at the highly decorated ceilings and long wooden tables lined with Germans drinking beer from litre tall beer glasses and ornamental steins.

Many of the drinkers were wearing lederhosen which Ian thought a little strange because if you were going for a drink with your mates in England on an ordinary Tuesday evening, you wouldn't dress up in traditional costume!

The Germans must like their uniforms, Ian thought. He was standing beside a table with four men sat opposite each other and Ian must have stared too obviously because one of them shouted at him.

"Ich bin kein tier."

Ian was startled and turned towards them.

"Ich bin Englander," he replied, not having understood what was said to him.

"Ah, my wife is Irish," the man retorted. "I said, I am not an animal."

"I'm sorry," Ian said and then looking around, he

continued, "I was just admiring the beer hall and all your wonderful outfits."

"Sit down," the man instructed.

Ian sat next to him. He was wearing a green felt hat with feathers on the top and a yellow rose on the side. He had a white shirt on and leather shorts with shoulder straps and a crossbar that were highly embroidered with flowers.

The man opposite Ian's new acquaintance started asking Ian questions and while Ian was trying to reply, the first man grabbed Ian's wrist and poured something on to the skin between Ian's thumb and forefinger. Ian wasn't really paying much attention and at first thought, he was just carrying out some form of ritual greeting but Ian soon saw the pyramid of brown powder on his hand. The two Germans indicated that Ian should sniff it and Ian realised it was snuff. Ian placed a tiny amount up his nose and felt the clearing sensation as though he had been breathing in menthol.

"Nein," the first man said and taking some snuff himself, he showed Ian how you should put your nose to your hand and then drag your nose across, sniffing at the same time.

Ian pretended not to understand. He hated anything to do with tobacco, so he stood up to walk away. The Germans made some dismissive gesture and growled a sort of 'Argh' which Ian thought was fair enough, but he just wanted to leave.

Ian pressed through the throngs of people, moving between the bar and the tables, past a brass band playing deafening music and headed for the exit. The waitresses wearing what he assumed was the female version of lederhosen and which he later found out was called dirndl, kept crossing in front of him to deliver fistfuls of beer and he couldn't help noticing that as one woman plonked down some beer glasses, her breasts were almost completely exposed. All the low-cut blouses were obviously part of the attraction.

Weaving through the packed room of revellers swilling vast amounts of beer Ian thought of a quote from Octavius Caesar in Shakespeare's Anthony and Cleopatra, 'I had rather fast from all four days, than drink so much in one.'

"My thoughts entirely," he said to himself as he managed to exit the building and take in some fresh air.

Diagonally opposite the Hofbrauhaus was a restaurant called Wirtshaus Ayingers which belonged to his hotel, so Ian sat down at one of the tables outside and ordered a small beer and the special of the day which was a veal and mushroom stew. It should have been delicious, but it was heavily salted and consequently, the ingredients were ruined. However, it enabled Ian to people watch for an hour or so before he returned to the hotel for an early night.

The next morning Ian went to the Munchner

Stadmuseum with the vague hope of finding the route to Manfred Fuchs's military records. There were lots of interesting photographs and posters and a potted history of National Socialism in Munich but when Ian asked the lady at the entrance desk if there were any archives on local SS officers, she looked down and shook her head. Ian then asked where one could find the military records of individuals who had fought in the war and again, she gave him an odd look and said she did not know. In England, Ian had simply filled in a request form and sent it to the Historical Disclosures department at the Army Personnel Centre in Glasgow to obtain his father's records but there seemed to be no such similar system in Germany or certainly not one that was willingly publicised.

Ian thought he would try a different tack and so he walked to Marienplatz and went into the Town Hall. A serious-looking middle-aged woman was standing behind a help desk.

"Hello, my name is Ian Sutherland," he said. "I had a friend who lived at Rubens Strasse 18 a few years ago but I have lost contact with him and I just wondered if you could look at the electoral roll and let me know who lives at the house now?"

The woman was silent, so Ian continued.

"His family may still be there or perhaps they have moved on and the new owners may know where they have gone."

"We do not have this," she replied in English.

"Do you know where I can get this information?"

"No."

Ian could tell from her look of disdain that he was getting nowhere so he wandered back into Marienplatz and sat down at a café opposite the tower of the neo-Gothic New Town Hall and ordered a coffee. He decided to listen to the famous glockenspiel at midday and watch the figures beneath the clock enact a joust and perform the Dance of the Coopers as it was one of those things every tourist to Munich had to do.

The ground floor of the town hall consisted of a row of archways fronting the square and behind each archway was a shop or café and Ian noticed that one of these individual units was the tourist information centre. Knocking back his coffee he went in and asked his two favourite questions, namely, how do you find out who lives at a certain address and where do you find out about the military records of an SS officer who came from and lived in the Munich area.

The man behind the counter looked at Ian in silence, turned away and came back with a leaflet. It was entitled 'Munich Walk Tours' and with a red pen he highlighted 'Third Reich Tour - Hitler's Munich.' This was not the answer to either question, but Ian thought it might be interesting, so he booked a place on the tour which started at 2.00 PM and was scheduled to last 2.5 hours.

Ian mooched around the town centre waiting for 2.00 PM. He drifted into an antique shop and seeing some old postcards asked if they had any of the Second World War. He received the usual negative response.

Ian was puzzled. Why wouldn't anyone talk about the war? Then it dawned on him. They lost.

The British were proud of their stoicism against all the odds and this was commemorated in virtually every town and city throughout the country with memorials and monuments, but the Germans were ashamed of their role in the war and they simply wanted to forget it.

Ian was musing over these thoughts as he stood outside the tourist information centre at 2.00 PM. The sun was directly overhead, and it was now very hot. This was more in line with what he had been expecting of Munich in August. Suddenly, he heard a girl's voice behind him.

"Mr Sutherland?"

Ian turned around and saw a beautiful young woman. She had shoulder-length naturally blonde hair and a lovely smile. She was wearing white shorts, a white T-shirt and a light blue, brushed cotton shirt on top, knotted at the waist. She wore white tennis shoes and short white socks.

"Yes, I'm Ian Sutherland," Ian replied hesitantly.

"I'm Sophie Mayer. I'm your guide. You're the only one booked on the tour today so shall we get started?"

"Yes, that's fine," Ian said as his thoughts started to race. Sophie's English was excellent, and she was very attractive!

They walked down Residenz Strasse to the Feldherrnhalle. The northern end of the hall comprised a large stone loggia with archways at the sides and steps at the front, leading up to a stage flanked by statues of lions. Ian stood at the top of the steps and with the lions either side of him, he looked down Odeansplatz. It was a very powerful image and Ian imagined Hitler addressing the crowds, inciting hysteria, as they screamed "Seig Heil" in response.

Sophie said this was where Hitler's people's revolution was stopped in 1923. Sixteen of his supporters were shot and Hitler was sent to prison. However, ten years later, when he came to power, he had a memorial erected "to the fallen of 9th November 1923" on the eastern side of the hall and every time someone passed by, they were made to salute in tribute. Apparently, some people avoided this by taking an adjacent side road.

"We call it a rat run in England," Sophie looked puzzled and unsure how to explain this, Ian continued. "Have you been doing these tours for long?"

"Oh, it's only a summer job," Sophie replied. "I'm a history student at the University. I am studying for a PhD on the White Rose resistance movement."

"What's that?" Ian asked.

"It was an opposition movement founded by Hans and Sophie Scholl and Professor Kurt Huber from the LMU and supported by many of the students."

"LMU?"

"Ludwig Maximilian University."

"What did they do?"

"They distributed anti-Nazi leaflets at the University."

"Did they do any good?" Ian asked slightly sarcastically and then wished he had bitten his tongue. They didn't exactly sound like the French Resistance, but Ian was worried that he had been a bit insensitive.

"I'll show you," Sophie said confidently.

They walked along the broad avenue of Ludwig Strasse towards the University and then Sophie turned left at Schelling Strasse and stopped abruptly in front of a red brick wall. The bricks were littered with bullet holes.

"This is where the students were shot. They were willing to give up their lives for what they believed in." Sophie's eyes were moist.

"I'm sorry," Ian said softly.

There was a sign on the wall which said 'Wunden der Erinnerung.'

"What does that mean?"

"Wounds of Memory."

Ian could see Sophie was upset.

"Let's go for a coffee," he said.

They found a café nearby and Ian told Sophie the story of John Field and how he was trying to find out more about Manfred.

"I will take you to the University. There is a permanent exhibition to the White Rose movement on the ground floor and we have a library full of archives," Sophie suggested, and Ian readily accepted.

The archivist at the University was called Birgit Scholz and Sophie was well known to her. Ian listened to them conversing in German. He couldn't understand what was being said but the body language was not hopeful. Sophie turned towards him.

"She says all the archives are about the White Rose movement. There isn't anything more general."

"One moment," Birgit said. She turned away and whispered something to a man who was sorting some papers on a desk behind her. She then came back to Sophie and on a piece of paper wrote the name, "Frau Eschenbach" and underneath she wrote a telephone number.

"Give this person a call," Birgit said. "She is a local historian and has lots of records about Munich during the war."

"Thank you." They both replied in unison and then they rushed out into the afternoon sunlight and stopped by the fountain in Professor Huber Platz.

"Can we ring her?" Ian asked.

Sophie looked at her watch. It was after 4.30 PM.

"I have to get to work," she said. "I work at a beer garden in the Englischer Garten from 5.00 PM to 8.00 PM and I have to get changed."

"But there's so much I need to talk to you about," Ian pleaded. Anxiety was written all over his face. Sophie looked pleased.

"Wait here. I will get changed and come back for you. If there is time, we can ring her from the payphone and then I will go to work and we can meet up afterwards."

"Where do you live?" Ian asked.

"Just there." Sophie pointed behind them towards the University.

"And where's the Englischer Garten?"

"Just there," Sophie said laughing as she pointed straight across the road in front of them.

Ian waited by the fountain for fifteen minutes. All sorts of confusing thoughts were swirling around his head. He liked Sophie and she could be a big help with his adventure. Maybe he could get her to come with him to Rubens Strasse 18 because if he did find any relations of Manfred Fuchs, he would need someone to translate.

Suddenly she appeared almost running towards him, smiling and looking excited.

She was wearing the traditional Bavarian costume called dirndl. Over a white blouse with a low-cut square neck and short puff sleeves, she wore a deep plum coloured pinafore dress which accentuated her breasts. It was tight around the waist had buttons up the front and was embroidered with flowers. Over the skirt was a purple apron although it was far too elaborate to call it that and she wore black high heeled boots which stopped just above the ankle. She looked fantastic.

"I've got five minutes," she said. "Here hold this."

Sophie passed Ian a plastic bag with an old-fashioned pair of low-heeled shoes in and then balancing herself by holding his shoulder she changed the boots for the shoes and handed him back the bag with the boots in.

"Look after these for me, will you? We'll ring Frau Eschenbach now and if she speaks English, I will make the introduction and leave you to speak to her while I go to work. You can meet me later to tell me how you got on?" She raised her voice slightly at the end of the sentence indicating she was seeking his agreement.

"Perfect," Ian replied.

They went to the payphone and dialled the number. Frau Eschenbach answered the phone by enunciating her name.

"Guten abend Frau Eschenbach. Ich bin Sophie Mayer. Sprechen Sie Englisch bitte?"

"Ja."

Sophie then explained she was a student at LMU and had been given Frau Eschenbach's name by Frau Scholz. She said she was standing next to an Englishman called Ian Sutherland and he would welcome the chance of speaking to her. Frau Eschenbach agreed, and Sophie passed Ian the phone and made to leave.

"Wait," Ian said anxiously. "Where will I meet you?"

"By the Chinese Tower," she replied as she rushed away. "Everyone knows where it is."

Ian explained to Frau Eschenbach that he was a lawyer and had property belonging to Manfred Fuchs from an estate in England and he was trying to find out a bit more about him before trying to track down the family.

"I don't have a file on him. I would remember the name but let me see if there are any details in my catalogue."

She seemed to be gone for ages and Ian had to put more money in the payphone several times but at least in Germany there was a display showing how much credit was left. Eventually, she returned.

"I have only brief details I'm afraid."

"Oh, thank you. That's fine. What are they?"

"Born: 22nd April 1914, in Munich.

Died: January 1945 in the Ardennes. Exact date unknown.

Occupation: banker.

Allegiance: NSDAP. Joined 1934.

Service: Waffen SS.

Rank: SS-Hauptsturmfuhrer. Captain in English.

Unit: SS Division Liebstandarte.

Battles: eastern front and western front.

Awards: Knight's Cross with Oak Leaves. That's it."

Ian was reeling still trying to take it all in.

"Did you say he was a banker?"

"Yes, it appears he started work at a bank after school,

joined the Nazi party aged 20 and then went into the SS probably at the start of the war."

"Thank you. You have been very helpful."

Ian put down the phone and looked at his watch. It was 5.10 PM and there was something he was desperate to tell Sophie. Frau Eschenbach did not, however, put down her phone. She cleared the line and dialled a London number.

Simon Black, head of the German desk at MI6 answered.

"Simon, it is Helga Eschenbach."

"Helga, how are you?" There was a rare tone of excitement in Black's voice.

"I am well, thank you but there is something you ought to know. I have just spoken with a young lawyer from England who wanted to know about Manfred Fuchs. He is here in Munich researching him."

"What did you tell him?" Black asked.

"Just the basics details from the catalogue.

"And his name?"

"His name is Ian Sutherland."

"Helga next time I am in Munich I will buy you a hot chocolate," Black said, referring to a private joke between them.

Black put down the phone and swivelled round in his chair so he could look out over the Thames. He didn't move for twenty minutes until his secretary interrupted his trance.

"Is everything all right, sir?" She asked with some concern.

"Everything is wonderful," he replied.

Chapter Eight

August 1987 – Munich

Ian was in high spirits. He was excited about seeing
Sophie again and he wanted to tell her about his latest
discovery, but he had over two and a half hours to fill first.
He decided he would check out where the Chinese Tower
was and then go back to the hotel for a shower.

The Englischer Garten was amazing; such a huge green
space in the heart of the city. There were people cycling,
people running and families just walking along enjoying
the sunshine. Within a short distance, he was surprised to
come across a river, Schwabinger Bach, just one of the
tributaries of the River Isar which ran through the park.
Children were swimming and splashing about in the water
which looked alpine clear. Ian knelt and dipped his hands
in it. The water was cold but not icy. What a wonderful
resource, he thought.

Ian carried on past a neo-classical folly on the top of a
hill but despite the panoramic views it doubtlessly offered,
he didn't climb up to it. He was a man on a mission. Then
in the foreground, he saw the unmistakable shape of the

multi-roofed Chinese Tower. He stopped and counted the tiers – there were five. Then he took his bearings and then headed back for the Platzl hotel as he didn't want Sophie to see him.

Ian still had over two hours to kill so he decided to try out the hotel gym. He didn't like lifting heavy weights because he did not want to carry unnecessary bulk just for the sake of it. Rather, he thought of the gym as somewhere to do a bit of circuit training as the games master called it at Sedbergh.

The hotel gym was a bit disappointing; small and lacking equipment. It was obviously more a matter of the hotel ticking a box than addressing the facility seriously. Nevertheless, Ian managed to do some planks and sit-ups for his core strength, some single-leg squats for balance and a series of six weights to exercise all the major muscles in the upper body.

Ian then took a little more care over his pre-dinner grooming having a slow close shave and a long hot shower. Doused in after-shave and wearing stone-coloured chinos, a navy-blue Ralph Lauren polo shirt and his chestnut, calfskin leather Church shoes, he made haste for his 8.00 PM rendezvous.

With the evening sun fading and families packing up their belongings, Ian meandered slowly along the footpaths leading to the Chinese Tower carrying Sophie's boots in the plastic bag she had given him. He was pleased with the boots. It meant she wanted to look her best for him and subconsciously, they formed a sort of bond between them guaranteeing a second meeting for their return.

He could see the green-painted tables and benches of the beer garden in the distance about half full of people chatting and drinking. He was relaxed and feeling good about himself when he saw Sophie stood beside a table with three young men, at least two of whom, were clearly inebriated and being rowdy.

Ian straightened and quickened his pace. The men were probably in their early twenties and he could see one of them, with straggly blonde hair, was clearly annoying Sophie.

If Ian had been a little closer and was able to speak German, he would have heard the man say: "show us your boobies," but luckily for the man, Ian did not hear this. Ian did, however, see him grab Sophie's arm. He speeded up and by the time Sophie had pulled away, Ian had gripped the man's wrist and forced it to the table.

"She's with me," he said.

The three men stood up to leave and made some sort of cooing noises and rude gestures, the blonde one holding on to his half-full litre glass of beer.

"You need to leave the glass," Sophie said to him.

The man raised his middle finger and then the three of them backed away noisily, holding onto each other and turning around shouting abuse, throughout which Ian stood like a physical block in front of Sophie, staring at them as they stumbled out of sight.

"Thank you," Sophie said softly.

Ian smiled at her. "Come on. Let's go for something to eat."

"Okay, we could go to Schwabing. There are lots of restaurants along Leopold Strasse."

Sophie took Ian a different route out of the Englischer Garten walking further north, along tree-lined paths lit by dappled sunlight.

A squirrel ran across the path in front of them and shot up the trunk of a horse chestnut tree.

"Squirrel!" Ian said automatically.

"In German, *eichhornchen*," Sophie replied. "How do you say it in English? Skirrel?"

"Squirrel." Ian enunciated carefully.

"Swirrel?"

"Squirrel!"

Sophie laughed and dropped her head onto his shoulder. "It is very hard to say in English."

They continued walking and almost instinctively their hands brushed against each other and immediately their fingers interlocked. Ian felt they became one, as though their bodies were joined in harmony. She didn't say anything, but Sophie was feeling the same. It was electric as though the same blood was flowing through both of them.

"How did you get on with Frau Eschenbach?"

"I've been meaning to tell you," Ian replied excitedly. "She said that Manfred Fuchs was a banker before joining the SS at the start of the war and Lord Granville was a banker. In fact, he owns a bank! He was the man who wanted alerting if Manfred was killed or captured. I can't help thinking there's a connection there, but I don't know what it is."

"It could be just a coincidence, or they might have had a business connection. Perhaps, Lord Granville's bank was lending the Nazi party money and Manfred was the link or maybe the Nazis were investing through him with the English bank. Who knows?"

"Someone knows," Ian said, "and I intend to find out."

They came out of the west side of the Englischer Garten and walked up Martius Strasse towards Leopold Strasse which ran north to south towards the centre of Munich. Ian saw a gold coloured Opel moving slowly up Martius Strasse, so he quickly crossed the road from left to right pulling Sophie with him. The car speeded up and as it went past it swerved at them and the man with straggly blonde hair leant out of the front passenger window and threw the beer glass, still containing some beer, at Sophie. It smashed on the pavement sending beer and glass everywhere.

Something inside Ian clicked. It was as though someone had flicked a switch. He looked at Sophie to check she was all right and then sprinted after the car. He could see that it was going to have to stop at the traffic lights at the top of Martius Strasse and it was in the lane to turn right so he ran diagonally towards a point on Leopold Strasse where he hoped he would catch it up. The driver didn't notice at first but then as he turned right, he saw Ian sprinting flat out across the corner of the broad pavements towards them. He pushed the accelerator to the floor and the tyres screeched as the car took off. Ian was running as fast as he could, his heart pumping hard and the adrenaline rushing through his veins. All the training paid off as his body synchronised its systems; rhythm, balance and power all working in perfect harmony. He reached the car just as it was picking up speed and, without stopping, he let his last stride hit the front passenger door with the flat of his heel. There was a loud bang as the metal indented. The driver slammed on the breaks and as the car stopped, the beer-throwing-lout flung open the door and jumped out of the car. He intended to fight but then he saw the look in Ian's eyes. It was a look of single-minded determination. It was a look that said, 'I'm going to win'.

Ian grabbed him by the lapels of his leather biker jacket and thrust him back against the car.

"I am British. Apologise." Ian said, pulling him down and forward, so he fell to his knees on the pavement.

"Entschuldigung. Entschuldigung." The man said, half standing up and hobbling backwards towards the car.

"Not to me; to her," Ian shouted, pointing at Sophie.

The man bowed at Sophie several times with his hands held in front of him as he walked backwards into the car, which, as soon as he was in, sped off.

Sophie ran up to Ian.

"Are you all right?" She asked with concern written all over her face.

"Fine," Ian replied, still pumping adrenaline. "Are you all right?"

"Yes."

They were both in shock. Somehow they decided on a restaurant adjacent to where they were standing although all Ian could remember about the meal afterwards was the scraping sound of metal chairs on the concrete pavement as diners moved out of their way as they went to sit down and the head waiter fussing to make sure the table was clean and to their satisfaction.

They were fairly quiet over dinner, but Sophie did agree to pick Ian up the next morning and take him to Rubens Strasse 18 in the hope of finding a connection with Manfred still existed.

"It's not unlikely," Sophie had said. "Germans keep property in the family for generations. They don't speculate like the English."

However, their minds were elsewhere. Sophie was stunned that Ian could charge a moving vehicle and actually come out on top. He made her feel safe and she had butterflies in her tummy. She was falling for him.

Ian was puzzled by his own behaviour. He was not angry. He had not lost control. It was calculated and concentrated aggression. He had never behaved that way before and he was not sure what it was. If John Field had been alive, he would have told him. It was the killer instinct – unleashed.

Chapter Nine

August 1987 – Munich

The next morning Ian was on the Opera House steps by 10.00 AM because Sophie had said it would be easier to get her car to Max-Joseph-Platz than try to navigate the one-way system and traffic to get to his hotel.

It was another beautiful day with clear skies and warm sunshine and Ian was raring to go. He was over the trauma of the night before and hoped Sophie would be all right too.

Predictably, she turned up in a VW Beetle, but it was a soft-top in a faded white colour with flower stickers on the doors and bonnet. Sophie gave him a lovely smile and he immediately knew she was fine. She was wearing a sleeveless, navy blue cotton summer dress with white spots, and the same tennis shoes she had worn the day before.

"Hop in," she said, pushing open the door and Ian did so after leaning forward to give her a kiss.

"Cool car," he said, strapping himself in.

"Well, all good German girls have to have one!"

The drive to Rubens Strasse took about half an hour along major roads with no sightseeing highlights but when they got to the residential area, Ian realised it was rather pleasant. They parked at the top of the road and before them lay an attractive avenue lined with elm trees on either side.

Ian had no clever ideas and was simply intending to knock on the door of number 18 and see what transpired but having parked at one end of the street, he and Sophie were able to walk down slowly and assimilate the surroundings first.

Number 18 sat behind metal railings and a well-trimmed hedge. Its gable end faced the street and was painted white with dark green painted shutters on the windows. On the first floor was a balcony with a dark wood balustrade and at its apex, the gable was wooden-cladded with a small square window. In other words, it was built in the traditional Bavarian vernacular and was rather pretty.

The surrounding houses were unique in style and quite substantial. This was obviously a prosperous area populated by the well-to-do. A young girl, perhaps eight years old, was cycling up and down the drive of the house opposite, each time venturing a little further out onto the pavement. She must have been watching Ian and Sophie and they must have been lingering a little too long outside number 18 because, when she gained the courage, she cycled up to them.

"Fraulein Fuchs isn't in. She's gone to the market to buy some rabbits, but she will be back this afternoon."

"Thank you," Sophie said. "We'll come back later. Bye-bye."

"Bye-bye," the little girl replied. "I'll tell her you called."

Ian and Sophie could hardly contain their excitement as they hurried back to the car.

"She said Fraulein Fuchs," Ian said. "That means Manfred has a relative still living in the house."

"Yes, and she said Fraulein which means she is an unmarried lady. It could be his sister or…" Sophie paused as she lingered on the last word. "No, I think sister is the most likely."

"What shall we do now? It could be hours before she gets back." Ian sounded frustrated.

"Get in," Sophie replied. "I will show you my Bavaria."

They drove for about an hour southwest of Munich through beautiful countryside and rich agricultural land. The sky was clear blue with just a few clouds dotted above the mountains on the horizon.

"This is fabulous," Ian said as the sun beat down on him and he watched the wind blow through Sophie's hair. "This is how I imagined Bavaria."

Sophie stopped the car in a car park in Andechs where she said there was a Benedictine monastery and they walked the short distance up the hill to what was one of the oldest churches in Germany. The views 180 meters above Lake Ammersee were spectacular and already the beer garden was filling up Germans ordering their litres of beer and knuckles of pork.

"This way," Sophie said as she led Ian around the church into some woods. The woods had wide paths and gushing streams and the tree canopy provided a welcome respite from the midday sun. They walked for 4km, all downhill, chatting and holding hands until they reached a village called Herrsching and from there they went on to the lake.

Ian could not remember being so happy. He was not expecting their woodland walk to end up at a lake and as they paddled barefoot in the cold clear water, they hung onto each other for balance because the pebbles were so difficult to walk on. They made it back across the pebble beach and lay down on some grass facing each other.

"I wish I'd brought my trunks," Ian said. "We could have gone swimming."

"That would have been nice," Sophie replied but she was looking pensive.

"Am I a bad person?" She asked.

"Pardon?" Ian was taken aback.

"Being German. Are we Germans a bad people?"

"No, don't be silly."

"But what about the war? There is always this

underlying guilt about the war. When we go abroad, people look at us suspiciously and I can tell they are thinking bad things about us."

"I don't think so," Ian said trying to reassure her. "Anyway, you cannot take the blame for a previous generation."

"But they were our relatives. We are descended from them."

"Yes, but the German economy was on its knees paying reparations for the First World War and Hitler offered a populist solution to peoples' problems. It wasn't surprising people voted for him and when people did, they didn't realise he was an evil madman."

"But the Germans did bad things in the war. Very bad things. Does that mean we are an evil people?" Ian sighed as he searched for the right words to set her mind at rest. "There are bad German people and good German people just as there are bad English people and good English people. For a while, the bad German people got the upper hand but love always conquers. Love always wins. The good people always win in the end and you're one of the good people."

"Do you believe that?" She persisted.

"Of course, I do. Anyway, I wouldn't be going out with you if I didn't". Ian stood up because his position was getting uncomfortable. Sophie stood up too, raised her head and looked into his eyes.

"Are we going out?"

"I hope so," Ian replied, hoping he hadn't revealed his intentions too quickly.

Sophie threw her right arm around his neck and then her left one and hanging onto him she kissed him. It was like no kiss he had ever had before. Ian felt Sophie needed him and he needed her. His hands were clasped at the base of her back. He pulled her in closer and they continued kissing.

They walked back into the village and Sophie popped into a small supermarket and bought some sandwiches made with local cheese and salami. Her mood was buoyant when they got the shuttle bus back to the monastery and while she found a table in the beer garden with a view of the mountains, Ian bought two half litres of the beer brewed on-site.

They were clearly just happy in each other's company and were giggling and laughing about nothing in particular when Sophie became serious again.

"You go home tomorrow."

"Yes, but I thought you might like to come to visit me in England sometime soon?"

Sophie smiled and lifting his hand up from the table she kissed it and held it to the side of her face.

"I'd like that," she said.

They got back to Rubens Strasse in the late afternoon and leaving the car in the same place as before, walked down to number 18. A stout lady in her late sixties was pruning some blackberry bushes in the garden. She was wearing a clerical grey linen dress and sandals.

"Fraulein Fuchs?" Sophie shouted over the garden gate.

The lady walked towards them. She had straight dark grey hair with a fringe which made it look more like a helmet, bare legs and forearms, and the strong hands of a butcher.

"She won't have any difficulty killing and skinning those rabbits," Ian whispered. Sophie elbowed him in the ribs.

"Ja, Ich bin Gertrud Fuchs," she replied.

"May I ask, are you related to Manfred Fuchs?" Sophie enquired in German with Ian just managing to follow.

"He was my brother."

"Can we ask you about him? My friend is a lawyer from England, and he has some of Manfred's property for you."

They were standing either side of the garden gate, but the gate was still firmly shut as Gertrud Fuchs had not invited them in. She stared at them suspiciously.

"No. Go away," she said.

"But we have his watch," Sophie said with a glance at Ian, to encourage him to show her. Ian pulled the watch out of his pocket and handed it to Gertrud. She glanced at it briefly and handed it back without saying anything, as she turned to walk away.

"Can we please just talk to you for a few minutes?" Sophie persisted.

"No," Gertrud replied firmly. "The war is over. Over, I tell you. I don't want to hear any more about the war. Now go away."

She turned her back on them and in desperation, Ian pulled Manfred's wallet out of his pocket.

"Wait," he shouted and opening the wallet he held it up so she could see the picture.

Gertrud turned back to face them.

"Do you know who this is?" Ian asked pointing at the picture of the woman and child. Gertrud frowned at him in disgust.

"Yes, she is English. Her name is Judith Granville. The child is called Freddie."

Chapter Ten

August 1987 – London

The next morning on the flight back to Heathrow, Ian chewed over the events of the last few days. His thoughts kept switching from Sophie and when he would see her again to Lord Granville and what he had discovered in Munich.

Presumably, Lord Granville had a daughter called Judith. Manfred was a banker, and this may have presented an opportunity which led to his relationship with Judith. Freddie was the likely product of that relationship. All of this would give Lord Granville a motive to take an interest in Manfred but nothing more.

Ian tried to shake himself out of it. "I am meant to be returning property not solving a mystery that isn't there," he said to himself.

But his mind kept drifting back. That Judith was English explained why the inscription on the watch was in English. It did not explain why she referred to Manfred as "Freddie" unless it was simply her pet-name for him.

Was Frederick Granville, the current chairman of the

bank, the Freddie in the photograph? He would be the right age because if he was born in 1940, he would be about 47 now. If he was Freddie, why was his surname Granville? He wouldn't want to use the name 'Fuchs' or admit to a father being an SS officer. On second thoughts, there was more to this than met the eye. At the very least, there had to be some sort of cover-up.

Ian was still mulling all this over as he walked through 'Nothing to Declare' into the public area of the airport where anxious parents and excited partners waited for their loved ones and professional drivers held up signs with their customers' names on.

Suddenly, Ian felt his personal space being invaded and as he looked up, he was confronted by two men in grey suits. They were both taller than him, a fact which was unusual in itself and this, along with their sober attire was somewhat intimidating.

"Mr Sutherland?" The tallest one asked. He was about six foot five with thick dark hair.

"Yes," Ian replied, looking puzzled.

"I'm Tom Hatchett and this is my colleague Tom Meeks. We are both with MI6." Both men discreetly pulled out some identification. "We would like you to come back to HQ to help us with some enquiries."

"Have I done something wrong?" Ian asked, remembering the fracas on Leopold Strasse.

"We don't think so, but you may be able to help us,"

Hatchett replied reassuringly.

"Okay," Ian said although the hesitation in his voice was clearly palpable.

The two Toms led Ian towards a black Rover 3500 V8, Hatchett walking in an uncoordinated fashion as though it was a struggle to control his hands and feet at the end of such long arms and legs. Meeks opened the back door for Ian and then got in beside him. He was about an inch taller than Ian with a slimmer profile and blonde curly hair.

"At least this will save me the train fare to Kings Cross," Ian said, trying to make light of the matter. "How long is this going to take anyway?"

"That depends on how long Niccolo wants to talk to you," Meeks said, laughing to himself.

Ian saw Hatchett glare at Meeks through the driver's mirror.

"Niccolo?" Ian said his voice rising to indicate a question.

"Don't worry about it," Hatchett replied. "It's a private joke. He's referring to Niccolo Machiavelli. You're going to meet Simon Black and Niccolo is his nickname because he's a bit Machiavellian I suppose."

Ian didn't reply as he was trying to remember his history. It was something to do with it being justified to do bad things if they were for the greater good.

He hadn't really observed where they were going or recognised any landmarks on the journey but now in the distance, Ian saw the distinctive chimneys of Battersea Power Station and soon they were crossing Vauxhall Bridge. The car turned left down Albert Embankment and then quickly left again and again into an underground car park. This is getting quite spooky, Ian thought.

Meeks got out of the car and held the door open for Ian. He clearly played second fiddle to Hatchett and seemed to have a more laid-back attitude.

"This way please," he said.

Ian followed him and Hatchett caught them up having parked and locked the car. He went ahead and opened doors as they went up through a series of concrete staircases managing the security systems to enable them to pass. Ian noticed he walked with his feet splayed and the heels on his rubber-soled shoes were worn down on the inside corner rather than the more usual outside corner.

"Just wait here please," Hatchett said.

The two Toms left Ian in a reception area that had the appearance of a three-star hotel. There was a blue patterned carpet, simple chairs covered with blue hessian cloth and a desk behind which sat a plump young receptionist with black hair and bright red lipstick.

Ian was kept waiting about five minutes and then a gaunt man with thinning brown hair in his mid-fifties appeared from behind a door to greet him. He was a little less than six foot, wore gold-rimmed spectacles which were, at least, fifteen years out of date and instead of a suit he was dressed in grey trousers and a fawn and brown hound's-tooth tweed jacket. He looked more like a schoolmaster from Sedbergh than a city professional except that the tweed jacket was a lighter weight than the Harris Tweed favoured by the Sedbergh clan. His unconventional attire immediately told Ian that there was something not quite British about him.

He came over to Ian and stood right in front of him. Ian stood up quickly.

"Simon Black. Welcome to MI6," he said, holding out his hand.

"Ian Sutherland. How do you do," Ian replied, giving him a firm handshake.

Black concentrated on Ian's eyes. "Tea?"

"Coffee please," Ian replied.

"Jane, two coffees please," Black said to the woman behind the desk. "Please follow me."

Ian followed Black up another flight of stairs into an office. Black sat behind a desk and indicated towards a seat at the other side of it.

"Have a seat," he said.

The office was quite large with a window overlooking the Thames. The walls were cream in colour and bare. On the wall opposite the window were bookshelves but they were just prefabricated plywood and filled with A4 ring binders, papers bound by a variety of methods and a few scattered books such as Hogan's Criminal Law. Behind the desk at which Black sat was a table with draws and that was it. No pictures on the walls, no photographs on the desk and nothing else which could be considered personal. But Ian got the impression it was Black's office. If it had been an interview room, it would not have a view, it would not be as large, and it would not have bookshelves filled with paperwork.

"Thank you for coming," Black said. His voice was soft, almost honeyed but there was a core of authority in it. He did not need to raise his voice to command.

"I didn't realise I had a choice," Ian replied.

Black half-smiled at him. It was not a friendly smile but more given in admiration, as though he was indicating he would have given a similar response if he had been in Ian's situation.

"My dear chap, don't worry yourself. We just want to ask you a few questions – that's all. I understand you have been enquiring after Manfred Fuchs?"

"How do you know that?" Ian asked.

"Frau Eschenbach mentioned it to me. I have had an association with her for a very long time."

The receptionist walked in with two coffees and placed them on the desk.

"Thank you, Jane," Black said to her.

The interruption had given Ian time to think.

"I still don't follow. I have been on holiday to Munich. I went on a Second World War tour of the city and ended up asking Frau Eschenbach a few questions about Manfred Fuchs, so how come I suddenly find myself at MI6 headquarters?"

"We have similar interests, Ian. I followed a similar path to you many years ago and I too ended up speaking with Frau Eschenbach. You see, Manfred Fuchs is a person of interest to us."

"He's dead," Ian replied. "How can you still be interested in him after all this time?"

"You're interested in him." Black stared at Ian and looked right through him. Ian didn't answer.

"Let me correct myself. Manfred Fuchs had connections. We are interested in his connections. Now, tell me why you are interested." Ian took a deep breath.

"I had a client called John Field, who died recently. He was a sniper in the Second World War. He shot Manfred Fuchs. He removed a Luger from the body along with Manfred's watch and wallet. Before he died, he asked me to trace Manfred's family and return his personal belongings." Ian's staccato sentences belied his underlying nervousness.

"And did you?" Black knew how to ask the right questions. Phrased differently, Ian could have given a more evasive answer, but this question went right to the point.

"No," Ian replied. "I found Fuchs's sister, but she showed no interest in the items. She said she would rather forget about the war." Ian was still holding back, and Black could see this. He swivelled his chair around to the table behind him, unlocked a drawer and pulled out an A4 brown envelope. He held the envelope up and peered inside at the contents. Carefully, he extracted a black and white photograph about A5 size and slid it across the desk to Ian.

"Do you know who this is?"

Ian looked at the picture. The face didn't have its red, watery eyes nor its permanently cross appearance. The hair wasn't thin and brushed back and the figure wasn't stooped but it was still the unmistakable image of Lord Granville.

"It's Lord Granville."

"Yes, it's Lord Granville stood outside his bank on Poultry in 1938. Do you see the heraldic shield affixed to the stonework by the entrance?"

"Yes," Ian replied, taking a second look.

"It marks the location of the bank because it started trading before street numbers were invented. Granville's bank is almost as old as the Bank of England. It was founded in 1689 and the shield is supposed to be a family relic from the twelfth century. It signifies strength, protection and family continuity.

"I can see that," Ian said, wondering where this was going.

"It's a private bank. Do you know what that means?"

Black's voice was rising. Ian wasn't sure if it was with anger or excitement.

"Erm, it's not a public company?" Ian feared this was a weak answer and he felt a bit stupid, but he wasn't entirely sure of the significance of Granville's being a private bank.

"It means it's an unlimited liability partnership. The bank is owned by partners and they lend their own money, so their personal assets are fair game for creditors. If the bank goes bust the partners lose everything." It was excitement. Black was animated with excitement.

"I'm afraid I'm struggling to see what any of this has to do with Manfred Fuchs or me," Ian said getting a little frustrated.

Black peered into the envelope and pulled out another photograph.

"Do you know who this is?"

The picture rang a distant bell, but Ian wasn't sure.

"No."

"It's Sir Oswald Mosley, leader of the British Union of Fascists. Now look again at the first photograph. Can you see Granville is waving good-bye to someone?"

Ian picked up the first photograph and studied it carefully. Granville had one hand raised; simply bent at the elbow with his hand at shoulder level. Walking away from Granville, the camera had caught the side profile of a smartly dressed gentleman. It wasn't the clearest likeness, but it was still the indisputable image of Sir Oswald Mosley. Ian let the photograph drop on the desk.

"It's Sir Oswald Mosley," he said.

"Sir Oswald Mosley was an aristocrat and a contemporary of Granville's although a couple of years younger. He was also a protectionist, nationalist, anti-communist, anti-Semite. Now, do you think any of these adjectives could be used to describe Lord Granville?"

"Perhaps," Ian replied.

"I agree, but they would hardly be fatal to the bank's reputation. Some of its customers might actually approve of such opinions. However, look at this.

Black pulled out another photograph this time of a wedding.

"This is a rare photograph of Mosley's second wedding. He married in secret in Germany in October 1936 at the home of Joseph Goebbels. Adolf Hitler was the guest of honour."

"So, I see," Ian said looking at the Fuhrer standing next to the happy couple.

"Now in 1940, Mosley went to prison and some time before that just after the first photograph was taken Granville severed all ties with Mosley. Being anti-Semitic is one thing but associating with a friend of Hitler's is another! If that got out it would have ruined Lord Granville's reputation and the bank."

"I'm sorry but I am still struggling to see the relevance

of all this."

"Have patience, Ian, have patience. I am not suggesting there was any financial link between Granville's bank and Mosley. Unfortunately, MI5 have all the intelligence on Mosley, and, in any case, Mosley was wealthy and spent a considerable amount of his personal fortune financing the BUF. I am merely saying they knew each other. But look at the photograph of the wedding again. Who do you think that is in the background?" Black had his index finger above the head of one of the figures.

Ian looked at the photograph. Mosley and his wife were centre stage with Hitler stood next to Mosley's new wife. In the background were lots of people all lined up, mainly men in sombre suits. Ian looked carefully. In his mind's eye, he was comparing one small image with another in a wallet.

"It's Manfred Fuchs," Ian replied.

"Exactly!" Black said excitedly. "Now you're going to have to concentrate."

Black pulled some flimsy sheets of paper from the envelope.

"These are carbon copies of Letters of Authority from Granville's bank. They are dated between 1936 and 1938. We got them from a member of staff who extracted them from the daybook so, unfortunately, they are not signed. Only the top copies would be signed, and only Lord Granville would be able to sign them, but they are his handiwork. Look who they are addressed to."

Ian flicked through the sheets of paper.

"Manfred Fuchs, at a bank in Munich," Ian paused. "I'm not sure what they mean though."

"Granville's had a Zurich branch. Just a single room office really but it enabled them to keep reserves at the central bank in Switzerland. Gold reserves. The Letters of Authority instruct the central bank to hold those reserves to the order of the German bank which Fuchs worked for rather than Granville's. Do you understand? The gold doesn't move but the ownership does." Black was in his element now.

"MI6 picked up that Fuchs was visiting London between 1936 and 1939. Until 1938 every time he visited, he collected a Letter of Authority."

"So, what you are saying is," Ian talked slowly but Black interrupted.

"Granville's bank was financing the Nazi party. Fuchs was the conduit through which the loans were facilitated. Then in 1938, Granville got cold feet. He could see war was coming and severed all connections. Hitler invaded Czechoslovakia in 1939 and misappropriated their gold. Then the debt was repaid. We've checked with the Bank of International Settlements and Granville's reserves fell between 1936 and 1938 and then all the withdrawals are replaced by one transaction just before the outbreak of war." Black continued.

"My belief is that Lord Granville is a fascist. He knew Sir Oswald Mosley and supported him politically if not financially. Fuchs was a banker and had joined the Nazi party in 1934. He attended Mosley's wedding in 1936, probably in some minor official capacity as it was held at Goebbels's home and perhaps that led to an introduction to Granville's. Either way, Granville then started lending the Nazis money or rather he provided the gold reserves which they could use as security for lines of credit.

In 1938 the writing was on the wall and the relationships were closed. Granville knew if the information became public, he and the bank would be finished. Fuchs joined the SS and Lord Granville went back into the Army (he had done a short-term commission after university) to do his bit for his country! He got an office job at MOD headquarters until 1945 when he was sent to Berlin for a year to help with the refugees flooding in from Eastern Germany."

Black pulled out a white handkerchief from his pocket and dabbed his brow. Ian noticed he had over-emphasized the word "help" at which point beads of sweat had formed on his forehead.

Ian's first instinct was to express amazement, but he didn't. He had already suspected that there must have been a financial link between Lord Granville and Fuchs and Black had just provided the detail. Why, Ian was not sure, but he thought he would play him at his own game.

This was exciting.

Ian reached into his pocket and pulled out Manfred's wallet. Opening it he pointed at the picture of Judith.

"Do you know who this is?"

Black looked puzzled. He wasn't used to having the tables turned.

"No," he replied.

"It's Judith Granville, the daughter of Lord Granville."

Ian could see the cogs turning but Black didn't say anything.

"And do you know who this is?" Ian asked pointing at the child. It was a rhetorical question and he didn't wait for an answer.

"It is Frederick Granville, the son of Manfred Fuchs, the grandson of Lord Granville and the current chairman of Granville's bank."

Black slumped back in his chair and for a moment, there was silence.

"Oh, my dear boy. You have done well. You have done very well."

"I need to verify this but I'm sure I'm right." Now it was Ian's voice that was elated.

Black was still sat back in his chair. He clearly did not know about the family connection between Granville and Fuchs but the look on his face was one of relief and joy. It was as though England had just won The Ashes.

"I think you should go to the Press with this," he said

at last. "I can put you in touch with the right people at The Times."

Ian pulled back. "My mission was to return the watch and the wallet. Why should I go to the Press?"

"Justice! The public has a right to know. The Granvilles present themselves as pillars of society when they are no more than a bunch of treacherous fascists." For the first time, Black's voice was raised.

"Why don't you go to the Press?" Ian asked.

"No. It wouldn't look very good coming from MI6. In any case, it's your story. You've got the beginning with John Field, the research in Munich and now the discovery. You can have these photographs if you like, as long as you don't say where you got them."

Ian pursed his lips and stroked his chin while he was thinking.

"I need to verify what I have told you and I want to think about it. Then I'll let you know."

Black sat up and his body language changed. He realised he had let his guard down which for him was unthinkable.

"Yes, of course, you must. Take your time and let me know when you are ready."

The air was fresh when Ian stepped outside. There was a nip in it too as a gentle breeze blew in from the North Sea, but Ian still decided to walk. He wanted to clear his head as he juggled facts and speculation.

The train from King's Cross was at 4.00 PM. Ian had to go to Anderson & Sheppard first and it was nearly 2.00 PM now, so the plan was to walk to the tailor and then get a taxi to the station. Vauxhall Bridge Road, though, was busy and the walk was unpleasant with the heavy traffic, so Ian cut in front of Buckingham Palace and went through Green Park to The Ritz. For a moment, Ian felt like going in just to sit down and relax but he kept going until he reached Savile Row. He felt a whole new chapter was opening up for him. He was now assisting MI6. He was a little in awe of Simon Black and while he had been warned about him, he felt he could handle things. He was, after all, a solicitor/spy.

He didn't really concentrate on the new suit. His mind was elsewhere so he was less effusive than usual with Finn and said the trousers were fine subject to a slight shortening being needed to the leg length as the waist was sitting a little lower than expected. Ian was similarly quiet with Danny for the jacket fitting until he noticed there was no pen pocket.

"Don't worry, Sir. I will add that later as it is a pocket within a pocket if you know what I mean," Danny explained.

"Sorry, Danny. I didn't mean to be sharp."

"That's all right, Sir. I appreciate the pen pocket is an important feature for you. The pen is mightier than the sword, as they say."

Ian looked up at the ceiling and for a moment was in a world of his own. He knew he was playing with fire, but the dancing flames were too alluring to ignore. Finally, he replied:

"You're right, Danny. A pen can be as sharp as a knife."

Chapter Eleven

August 1987 – North Yorkshire

The first week of Ian's holiday was over. He dragged himself out of bed on Saturday morning and looking in the mirror, realised how tired he was. It wasn't surprising really. He had travelled to Munich, started a relationship with Sophie and been questioned by MI6 to name just three of the highlights from the previous week.

Unshaved and bleary eyed, Ian threw on his tracksuit and walked to the bottom of Valley Drive where there was a small café on the corner of Crescent Road. He felt it was his 'local' and this early in the morning he could get away with looking dishevelled.

"Fresh orange juice, espresso and poached eggs on toast please," he said to the waitress.

Sipping his coffee, Ian thought about things carefully. He wanted to return the watch and the wallet and the obvious recipient of these items, should be Judith. However, he didn't want to rush in. He wanted to prepare the ground first and get an idea of who he would be dealing with. He didn't have much appetite for the newspaper idea, regardless of how exciting that might seem. Most of all, though, he wanted to discuss everything with Sophie or, better still, see her.

Refuelled with caffeine, Ian went back to his flat and telephoned Sophie. He was nervous as he waited for her to answer. She might be out. She might have thought theirs was just a holiday romance. She had said she would like to come to England, but this might be much sooner than she had in mind.

"Hello," Sophie said as she answered the telephone. Ian's heart raced as he heard her voice.

"Hello. How are you?"

"I'm okay but I'm missing you." Ian's heart leapt for joy.

"I'm missing you too," he said, "but you won't believe what's happened to me since I last saw you."

"What?" Ian could sense her concern.

"I've been questioned by MI6."

They then chatted for over an hour, although the time just flew by. Ian described the interview at MI6 headquarters and Sophie agreed to fly to Heathrow on Monday and get the train to York as the flights were more frequent than those to Manchester.

"Be careful," she said. "I don't like the sound of that Simon Black. I don't trust him." This was the second warning Ian had received about Simon Black but for some strange reason, Ian found himself bewitched. It was like playing with a snake knowing it was dangerous but hoping you could avoid a bite.

Sunday was a joy of preparation as Ian washed his clothes, cleaned the flat and stocked up the fridge in anticipation of Sophie's visit. He put Manfred and the Granvilles to the back of his mind and thought only of Sophie and how much he liked her.

When Sophie stepped off the train at York Station Ian wasn't disappointed. Her hair had been cut a couple of inches off the shoulder. It was neither straight nor curly but looked tousled with a blunt edge around the neckline. She looked natural and used make-up sparingly. Her blonde hair was offset against a black leather jacket which she was wearing over black and white checked capri pants and a fitted white cotton jumper. To complete her outfit, she wore kitten heel slingbacks and carried a small black Chanel handbag. Ian noticed the flatness of her stomach and the curvature of her thighs and realised that she was not only beautiful but athletic too.

Sophie threw her arms around Ian and this was the bit he liked most. She was tactile, warm-hearted and loving.

Ian held open the door of the E-type to let her in.

"Is this yours? She asked, caressing the metallic paintwork with her hand.

"Yes, nice, isn't she?"

"She's beautiful," Sophie replied. Ian thought about but avoided the obvious response.

"I've booked you into a country house hotel in the village of Markington as all the hotels in Harrogate are a bit corporate; full of people going to the Conference Centre. It's called Hob Green."

"It's not too far away?" Sophie asked anxiously.

"No, less than eight miles. I thought we could have dinner there together tonight and then tomorrow; I have a plan. I want to go to Harrogate Library and look at the newspaper reports of weddings and perhaps christenings. For a family like the Granvilles, these must have made the headlines."

Hob Green was set in several hundred acres of farmland and as the Jag swung through the entrance gates, a squirrel shot up one of the walnut trees that lined the drive.

"Eichhornchen!" Sophie exclaimed laughing as she had managed to say it first. Suddenly, the canvas roof of the car was showered with a fall of walnuts and Sophie jumped at the sound of the impact.

"What's that?"

"It's the squirrels," Ian replied. "They're attacking us."

They fell into the reception laughing, Sophie holding on to Ian's arm and dropping her head on to his shoulder. Ian liked it when she did that.

The manager of the hotel greeted them with a glass of champagne. Ian glanced across at the bottle and was relieved to see it was real – Lanson Black Label to be precise. Fine as an early evening aperitif.

Sophie went up to her room to bathe and change for dinner while Ian wandered on to the terrace with his champagne.

He sat down and looked over the gently undulating fields to some woods in the distance. The only sound he could hear was the grazing of sheep. It was so peaceful; idyllic in fact. Everything was as nature had intended, he thought.

The sheep were getting closer, only prevented from reaching him by the ingenuity of a ha-ha and as they did so the sound of their grazing got louder. They sounded like an army marching towards him as they methodically ripped the grass from its roots but there was something soul restoring about the rhythm. To the beat of their drum, Ian felt recalibrated and ready for action.

It was seven o'clock when Sophie came downstairs as she had been over an hour getting ready, but it was worth the wait. Ian was stunned when he saw her. She looked beautiful.

She was wearing a black silk dress in the style of a shirt with long sleeves and buttons down the front. The collar was open, and she wore a simple silver necklace around her neck and a broad black belt around her waist. The length was short, and her legs looked amazing in the nude-coloured sheer stockings and black high-heeled shoes.

"You look fantastic," Ian said quietly as he took her

hand.

"You do too," she replied, which took Ian by surprise. He was not used to receiving compliments and he felt slightly underdressed in his blazer and stone-coloured chinos.

They went into dinner, but they had both lost their appetites. They were pent up with passion, both trying to suppress their feelings in this public arena. Sophie kept tugging at the bottom of her dress to pull it down as every time she moved the top of her stockings and suspender belt straps were revealed. Ian was transfixed by the way the silk dress clung to the curves of her body. He wanted her more than he had ever wanted a woman before, and she wanted him.

They had just one glass of wine each. They enjoyed the starter but as their desire intensified, they both struggled with the main course and without conferring they declined dessert and coffee.

"I'm going up to bed," Sophie said feigning tiredness.

"I'll see you to your room," Ian replied automatically.

They walked up the stairs in silence, a soft mushroom coloured carpet underfoot amplifying the atmosphere of anticipation. Sophie's room was number 11.

"It has a four-poster bed," she said abstractedly as she opened the door.

"Oh," Ian replied as he followed her in to have a look.

He pushed the door to behind him and Sophie turned to

face him. With her soft blue eyes, she looked into his and he kissed her. She stepped back towards the bed and Ian held her arms and pushed her gently as her body willingly folded on to the side of the bed. Ian undid the buttons nearest her neck, and she swung her feet on to the bed. He got on beside her and they pulled and tugged at each other's clothes as they kissed and searched for their most sensitive areas.

With the curtains open and the moon providing just the right amount of light, they made love. Passionately, lovingly and desperately giving themselves to each other, holding each other as they shuddered and fell apart complete.

Exhausted, they fell asleep, but Ian woke with a start, perhaps an hour or so later. He looked at his watch. It was nearly midnight.

"I've got to go," he said.

"No, stay," Sophie pleaded.

"No, I must go," Ian replied, pulling on his trousers. "I don't think the hotel would be too happy if I stayed and I will need some fresh clothes in the morning. I'll pick you up tomorrow." He kissed her good-bye and hurried out the door.

The next morning at breakfast, Sophie was having palpitations. She wasn't sure if she had done the right thing and now, she was sat all alone. She needn't have worried. She heard Ian's voice as he greeted the manager and then he appeared in the doorway looking for her table. She saw him first. He was wearing a blue cotton crew neck jumper and jeans. He looked strong and his hair was freshly washed. He walked over and kissed her.

"Hello, my love."

Sophie blushed and looked down at her plate.

"What lovely eyelashes you have."

"Stop it!" She said as she made a friendly swipe at him across the table.

Ian had a coffee with her and then they set off to Harrogate Library. It had a small but impressive neo-classical stone frontage set back from Victoria Avenue with a broad pavement in front. They went inside to witness a hive of inactivity. Some elderly men were sitting reading newspapers and other people were perusing the content of the shelves while an orderly queue waited to check books out or return them.

Ian and Sophie waited their turn and after a few minutes, a trim and prim librarian reflected on their enquiry, looked over her glasses and directed them to the first floor.

Upstairs, Ian found a slim, middle-aged man who seemed to be filing some papers.

"Hello," Ian said. "I wonder if you can help me. I want to look up details of a wedding which took place in 1939 or perhaps 1940. It involved a local aristocratic family so I am sure there must have been some newspaper coverage and I was hoping you might have some archives with the relevant information?"

"Yes, I'm sure we will have," the man replied. "We have the Harrogate Advertiser on microfilm."

Ian was taken aback at the positivity of the reply; so different from his experience in Germany.

"Can I have a look please, say at 1939?"

"We have a biographical index," the man replied.

"What does that mean?" Ian asked.

"Well you look up the name you are interested in and it gives you the relevant references."

Ian looked at Sophie. He couldn't believe how simple this was proving.

"Sorry, what's your name?" Ian asked.

"Adam."

"Adam, we are very grateful for all your help. We want to look up the name Judith Granville."

"Let's have a look," Adam said, swelling with pride.

He walked off to some shelves just a few feet away and came back with a large leather-bound book.

"Judith Granville, you say. Here we go. There are two entries; a wedding in 1939 and an announcement of birth in 1940. If you would like to follow me, I will show you how to view the microfilm."

Ian and Sophie scrolled through the material until they reached the first entry. It was headed:

Mr D Moor and The Hon J Granville. Beneath that it said:

The marriage took place on the 30th September 1939 at Christ's Church, Harrogate between David, son of Mr and Mrs Moor of The Old Lodge, York and Judith, only daughter of Lord and Lady Granville of Florin Hall, Harrogate.

"So, they got married just after the start of the Second World War," Ian said to Sophie.

Quickly, they moved on the next entry. It read:

David and Judith Moor Granville are delighted to announce the birth of their son Frederick Moor Granville, born on 30th March 1940 at 10.30 in the morning weighing 5lbs 4 ounces.

"That's only six months after the wedding," Sophie said.

"I know but hang on I've got an idea." Ian went back to Adam.

"Adam, that's great thank you, we have found out the first bit of information we needed but now we could do with inspecting the Electoral Register. Do you know where we can find a copy?"

"We have a copy here," Adam replied. What do you want to know?"

Ian just couldn't believe his luck.

"I would like to look up the address for Judith Granville and David Granville although I don't understand why they are not called Moor because the wedding announcement refers to David Moor marrying Judith Granville but the announcement of birth refers to them as David Moor Granville and Judith Moor Granville."

Adam pulled a ring binder from behind the desk and started turning over the pages.

"That's not necessarily unusual," he replied. "You said they were a local aristocratic family. Well, if there was no male heir and David Moor was a commoner, he may have taken her name. It can sometimes even be a legal condition of the Marriage Settlement."

"That would explain it," Ian said. "It does say that Judith is the only daughter, although I suppose that doesn't exclude a son."

"Here we are. Judith Granville. Her address is: The Stables, Florin Hall, Harrogate. It's a few miles out but it's a Harrogate postcode. Nothing for David Granville, I'm afraid. I'll try David Moor." Adam flicked through some more pages. "Yes, David Moor of Farthings Cottage, Bishop Monkton."

Ian shook Adam's hand. "Thank you so much. We really are very grateful."

In a celebratory mood, he turned to Sophie. "Come on, let's go to Bettys."

Bettys was synonymous with Harrogate and Harrogate was synonymous with Bettys. Founded in 1919 by a Swiss chocolatier, Bettys Café was housed in prestigious premises in the town centre overlooking The Stray. In Ian's opinion, it was the best café in the country. Its setting was just right and the quality of its creations superb. It was an experience Ian wanted Sophie to savour and luckily, they got a window seat looking across Montpellier Parade towards The Stray.

They both ordered cappuccinos and Sophie succumbed to the recommendation of a slice of the Grand Cru Chocolate Sachertorte made with dark Swiss chocolate and an apricot filling. To keep her company, Ian ordered a chocolate brownie.

"What I would like to do is get David Moor's telephone number from directory enquiries and see if he will let us pay him a visit," Ian said while they waited for their coffee and cake to arrive.

"What is it you want to know from him?" Sophie asked.

"Well, we know from MI6 that Manfred was visiting England until just before the start of the war. If the baby had been carried full term, that would give a conception date in June 1939 because it was born in March 1940. Judith married David Moor in September and the baby was born six months later so she must have already been pregnant when she got married unless the baby was premature, and the low weight suggests that. The fact that David and Judith now live at separate addresses would indicate they have got divorced. I just think we should get some of the background information out of David before we approach Judith."

Their coffees arrived and then their cakes. Sophie's was a formidable wedge of rich chocolate and sponge whereas Ian must have ordered something meant for a child because the chocolate brownie had a marzipan face of a fox on the top. Sophie laughed and pointed at the fox.

"In German, Fuchs," she said.

For a moment, they looked at each other in silence. It was said light-heartedly but somehow brought them back to reality. Ian looked at Sophie's hand, the nails painted with an attractive grey varnish and he lifted it to his lips and kissed her.

A look of concern flashed across her face.

"Foxes are cunning," she said. "It is dangerous what you are doing."

"Don't worry," he said, letting his eyes divert across The Stray. "To paraphrase Matthew's Gospel, I will be as cunning as a fox but as innocent as a dove."

He hoped his show of confidence would put Sophie's mind at rest. It hadn't worked on his own.

Chapter Twelve

August 1987 – North Yorkshire

The next morning Ian and Sophie drove to Bishop
Monkton, a pretty village with a stream running through
its centre, about six or seven miles north of Harrogate.

David Moor had sounded affable over the telephone
and readily agreed to meet them. Ian had simply said he
was a lawyer and wanted to come and chat about a client
who had a tenuous link to the Granville family, and this
seemed to do the trick.

Farthings Cottage was built of limestone with a soft
pink pantile roof. It looked like a house drawn by a
child because at the front it had four Georgian style sash
windows with a door in the centre and a chimney at each
gable end. Otherwise, it had a very plain appearance. It
would not, however, be a cheap property. It had a stone
wall fronting the road, a sweeping drive and a large back
garden including an orchard. This was fenced off from
the rest of the garden and Ian could see some fluffy white
hens pecking at the ground beneath the trees.

They were greeted by a well-fed yellow Labrador

which pottered up to them with a woof *hello* and a wagging tail. Ian bent down to stroke her.

"Careful, she'll lick you to death," David Moor bellowed as he appeared around the corner.

"Hello, I'm Ian Sutherland and this is my assistant Sophie Mayer," Ian said, shaking hands.

"David Moor. Pleased to meet you. Come on in."

They went through the front door into a narrow hallway and from there into a square sitting room overlooking the back garden.

"Coffee?" David asked. "I've got the pot on."

"Yes please," they both replied in tandem.

The Labrador had followed them through to the sitting room and curled up in her basket. David had gone through to the kitchen and Sophie was perched on the floor stroking the dog.

"What's her name?" Ian called through to the kitchen.

"Clover," David shouted back. "She's my lucky four-legged clover but don't tell her that!"

David brought through a tray of coffee and biscuits. He was a large man, in his early seventies, somewhat overweight, balding and with a thick double chin. He was wearing yellow corduroy trousers and a checked Viyella shirt.

"Help yourselves," he said, throwing a biscuit to Clover who caught it in mid-air with a snap that a crocodile would be proud of.

"Thank you for agreeing to see us..." Ian said but David cut him off before he could finish.

"My pleasure, old boy. I don't get many visitors nowadays. What can I do for you?"

"I wanted to ask you about the Granville family and, in particular, Judith Granville. I think you were married to her and are, perhaps now divorced?" Ian dragged out the last three words slowly, not wishing to cause offence.

"You do your homework! Yes, we were married; a long time ago. We got divorced just after the war."

Ian realised that to get the information, he would have to give some first and it was only fair. The man had a right to know why they were in his house. In any case, by giving information, Ian hoped to gain David's confidence which could make him more open in his response.

"I had a client who was a sniper during the war. In 1945 he shot an SS officer called Manfred Fuchs."

David Moor sat bolt upright.

"Now there's a name from the past!"

"I thought you might know it," Ian paused while David adjusted his seat. "My client was called John. He went up to the dead body and removed Manfred's Luger to keep as a trophy item. There were orders to identify who had been shot so he also removed his nametag, wallet and watch."

"I see," David said, expressing disapproval.

"In the wallet was a photograph of a woman and child." Ian pulled out the wallet from his pocket and handed it, open, to David. He looked at it briefly and sank back in his chair.

"Good God."

"I think the lady might be Judith Granville and the child her son Frederick?"

"That's right," David replied, still looking shocked.

"The watch has some value and just before he died, my client asked me to return it to Manfred's family together with the wallet." Ian handed the watch to David who looked at it and automatically turned it over.

"Always yours, Judith. Well, that sums it up nicely!" David said with a hint of bitterness in his voice.

"I went to Germany, to the address on the ID card and with Sophie's help spoke to Manfred's sister, Gertrud but, sadly, she didn't want anything to do with it. It was Gertrud who suggested that the photograph was of Judith."

Ian wasn't sure whether to stop there or continue. He didn't want to frighten David but, on the other hand, this might prompt him to be more forthcoming.

"When I returned from Germany, I was questioned by MI6. They had been alerted that I was looking into Manfred's background, just out of interest I hasten to add. MI6 suggested there may have been a financial link between Granville's bank and the Nazi party and Manfred was the conduit through which such business was conducted."

Ian paused for a response and David obliged.

"Doesn't surprise me but what do MI6 want with all this after all this time?"

"I don't know," Ian replied. "I was going to give the watch and wallet to Gertrud, but it now seems like Judith would be the more appropriate person. I was wondering if you could tell me what she was like and whether she would welcome a visit from me?"

"What's she like! Huh, that's a good one. How long have you got?"

"We've got as long as you like." Ian looked at Sophie who was getting a bit stiff sitting on the floor, so she left the dog and sat beside Ian on a small two-seater sofa.

"After Agricultural College at Cirencester, I came back to Yorkshire to run the mushroom farm on the Granville Estate. Lord Granville was a hard taskmaster, but I'd always admired Judith from a distance. She didn't want anything to do with me. Then, suddenly, she started paying me attention. You could say she threw herself at me. We started going out and before you knew it, she said she was pregnant, and we were rushed down the aisle. The baby came six months later, and she said it was premature. That's when I knew it wasn't mine. It was a big healthy baby, but they shaved three pounds off the weight for the announcement in the paper."

"So, what happened next?" Sophie asked.

"I tried to make the most of it. She admitted Manfred was the father, but she became completely cold towards me once the baby was born. The marriage just became a business transaction. I ran the mushroom farm and she ran the household."

"I'm sorry to hear that," Ian said.

"Anyway, towards the end of the War, she got a letter from him. He said he wanted her back and wanted to start a new life with her in Argentina. She was all for it, but you can imagine Lord Granville went berserk."

"And then Manfred was killed?" Ian interjected.

"Yes, and then Manfred was killed so that put the kibosh on their plans."

"Was it after that you got divorced?" Sophie asked.

"Pretty much. We had nothing in common and were just making each other miserable. I was given the mushroom farm to keep me quiet." Then he quickly added.

"It's only ten acres but has lots of prefabricated buildings."

"Moors Mushrooms!" Ian exclaimed as a penny dropped. Moors Mushrooms was a well-known brand of mushrooms.

"Yes, I became Moors Mushrooms. Remember the adverts? *We get up early and search through the woods.* Well, we did get up early and search through the sheds! Low margin though; just about scraped a living."

"And you never remarried?" Sophie asked, feeling sorry for him.

"No, it's just me and Clover and the three before her

but she'll be the last. I just want to live long enough to see her out."

"Oh, don't say that!" Sophie replied with alarm.

"Well, I'm diabetic. That's why I couldn't join up and farming was a reserved occupation. So, I stayed at home and ended up with Judith. Fighting Hitler might have been easier!" They all laughed and then Ian pressed on.

"I got a bit confused by the whole name thing because your surname was Moor and then I think you became Moor Granville, unhyphenated and now you're Moor again."

"Simple enough. Lord Granville insisted I took their name when we got married and I changed it back when I got my freedom. It worked for him though because now he has an heir called Granville. You see my name was insignificant and that's how they made me feel. That's why I called this place Farthings Cottage, as a bit of a joke, a farthing is insignificant to a florin."

"Florin?" Sophie asked, missing the point.

"Florin Hall. That's where they live; a stately pile not far from here."

"And what about the financial link with the Nazi Party? Do you know anything about that?" Ian asked.

"I'm afraid not. I was just a small cog in the wheel. They would never discuss business with me unless it was about mushrooms."

Ian was worried they might be overstaying their

welcome and that this was turning into an interrogation although David did not give any such indication. Nevertheless, he thought they should stop while ahead.

"Finally, how do you think Judith will respond if I ask to visit her? I would like to give her these." Ian said, picking up the watch and the wallet which David had placed on the coffee table.

"Give her a call. I'm sure she will agree to see you if you say you have some of Manfred's belongings to return."

"Well, thank you for having us," Ian said. "You've been a great help and I will try to make contact with Judith."

They all shook hands good-bye and Sophie bent down, placed her hands over Clover's ears and kissed the top of her head.

"And it was nice to meet you too," she said.

Ian could see Sophie was looking a little sad and he wanted to cheer her up.

"Do you want to drive?" He asked as they approached the Jag.

"Really?"

"Of course." Sophie ran around to the driver's side and jumped in before Ian could open the door for her.

"Where are we going?" She asked.

"I thought we could go to Fountains Abbey for a picnic."

Sophie clapped her hands. "How exciting; I love

picnics."

"You haven't seen what I've made yet," Ian said sarcastically.

With Ian's guidance, Sophie took the back road from Bishop Monkton to Ripon and then via Studley Roger to the deer park. She had obviously been mulling over things because she suddenly came out with a definitive statement.

"I don't like the Granvilles," she said. "I do not think they are a very nice family."

Ian didn't bother replying because he was just enjoying the moment. It was a lovely summer's day and he had put the roof down on the Jag so they could make the most of the sunshine. His eyes were fixed on Sophie and as she concentrated on her driving, Ian watched her hair blow in the wind. It was completely natural, not bleached blonde but the colour of straw. Her eyebrows were the same colour and her blue eyes were narrowed as she stared into the sunshine. And then, there were her soft pink lips. She was truly beautiful, and Ian just wanted to kiss her.

With Ripon Cathedral in their rear view, Sophie drove through the deer park but instead of turning left to the lake Ian asked her to turn right and following an ever more contorted route with the road disintegrating into a track she stopped at a little-used cricket ground for the village of Studley Roger. It was set in its own amphitheatre formed by a circular mown field bounded by oak and chestnut trees. In the heart of one of the National Trust's most popular attractions, they were completely secluded.

"That was fantastic," she said as the car stalled to a halt.

Ian spread a car rug on the grass and carried the icebox from the car. Opening it, he took out two champagne glasses wrapped in a tea towel and half a bottle of Veuve Clicquot.

"What are we celebrating?" Sophie asked as she sat down on the rug.

"You," Ian said softly.

"Me? Why me?"

"Because I love you."

Sophie's eyes filled with tears and she threw her arms around Ian's neck and kissed him so hard he fell back almost spilling the champagne.

"I love you too," she said.

They drank their champagne and did their best not to make a mess with Ian's choice of picnic food which consisted of a baguette, a tub of prawns in Marie Rose sauce and fresh strawberries. Ian had also brought a flask of fresh coffee but no mugs, so they had to share the top of the flask, which was actually quite romantic.

"I go home tomorrow," Sophie said sadly.

"Yes, but I will come to London with you on the train and try to meet up with Simon Black. I'm going to tell him I will return the watch and the wallet to Judith and that's me out of it. I'm not going to have anything to do with his leak to the Press idea."

"I agree with you, but will he be all right with that?"

"He will have to be. He has no choice," Ian replied.

Sophie put that worried look on her face again.

"But if he can't make you do his bidding, what will he do instead?"

Chapter Thirteen

August 1987 – London

Simon Black told Jane he was taking the afternoon off as he hurried out of MI6 headquarters and caught the bus from Vauxhall Bridge to Piccadilly Circus. He preferred taking the bus as he didn't like the Underground, which he considered dirty and claustrophobic.

He usually walked from his home in Marylebone to Piccadilly Circus because he enjoyed the exercise at the start of the day. It was slower, but that was simply a matter of time management and he found it amusing watching everyone rush about in a state of anxiety, always blaming their lateness on the traffic when, in reality, they only had themselves to blame.

In the evening he also disembarked at Piccadilly Circus unless the weather was bad in which case, he might stay on for a couple of extra stops to Oxford Circus. He didn't mind a bit of rain, though, and he found Central London quite atmospheric at that time of day as the sunset on the horizon.

Today, he had to get off at Piccadilly Circus because

he wanted to go to Fortnum & Mason. He was excited to have received the telephone call from Ian because he wasn't expecting a response so soon and now, after years of waiting, his master plan was coming together.

Black had invited Ian to afternoon tea at his home, saying it would be more private, so he needed to buy some appropriate delicacies to tempt him with. He settled on an Orange, Earl Grey and Cardamom Loaf Cake and some Teacup Fancies.

It took Black just under thirty minutes to walk to Montagu Square via New Bond Street, Oxford Street and Gloucester Place. He would often vary the route slightly to take in different points of interest, but today, he didn't want to dawdle.

Montagu Square was one of the most sought-after addresses in Marylebone, especially amongst the professional classes. An oblong railed garden formed a square around which many Georgian houses had been converted into luxury apartments. The garden with its mature trees and pretty flowerbeds interspaced with benches provided a peaceful sanctuary in this thriving metropolis and this was the reason Black had made it his home.

Black climbed the stairs to his first-floor apartment, placed the cakes on the kitchen table and put his jacket over the back of a chair. He then went over to the record player in the sitting room and put on some music. Black smiled with self-satisfaction at his selection. He had chosen one of Chopin's nocturnes; Opus 9, Number 2 in E Flat Major, to be precise. Chopin did not invent the nocturne but rather developed and popularised a form of music first conceived by an Irish composer called John Field. No one would appreciate the association with the composer's namesake which had driven his choice of record and he marvelled at his own intelligence.

Back in his small galley kitchen, Black took a piece of leftover quiche out of the fridge together with a tomato and having poured himself a sherry, sat down in his favourite chair, by the bay window, overlooking the garden.

A sparrow hawk had pounced on a collared dove and was now ripping the flesh from the carcass looking up with every mouthful in case of danger. It had piercing black and yellow eyes and the way it kept looking up made Black think of a sniper's telescopic sight seeking and feeding back vital information.

Black allowed his mind to drift from John Field to his own experiences in the Second World War. He stretched for a cheap, tin money box from a nearby bookcase, unlocked it and stared at the contents. He took out his birth certificate and quietly spoke out his name. He was born Simon Schwarz in Konigsberg, Eastern Prussia in 1933.

He had one photograph, taken with his father in the botanical gardens when he was aged four. He had looked at it many times and assumed he had been happy, but the truth was it was too long ago to remember.

The bad times were not so easily erased. His father was a Jew and taught music at the Albertina until Jewish academics were ejected from the university in 1934. This may be where his love of music came from although he would not want to admit that.

His mother was a Lutheran Protestant and somehow, they had made ends meet until, in 1937, it had all become too difficult at which point his father left for New York. He said he would send for them but the next thing the young Simon knew, a German Officer had moved into the family home and he never saw or heard from his father again.

Horst was a strict man, but he did not mistreat Simon, and to Simon's relief, Horst was away most of the time, fighting Russians until he lost a leg during the Battle of Stalingrad. He came home for a while and they thought his fighting days were over but then got called back to the eastern front where he was killed almost as soon as he arrived. That was in late 1943 and in the intervening years he fathered five children. Amazingly, Simon's mother had given birth annually, providing children for The Reich in accordance with Nazi Party policy.

Black broke off some quiche with his fork, put it in his mouth and chewed slowly. Maybe his mother did it to survive but after Horst was killed, she *married* again, this time to an older man who was a professor at the University. Klaus had known Simon's father and he was kind to Simon but in the early part of 1945, he too was killed this time by the Allies in a bombing raid. Simon's mother though was pregnant again!

Truth is stranger than fiction, Black thought as he took a sip from his glass of sherry. In the space of six or seven years, his mother had lost three *husbands* and produced six children. No one would believe it if he told them which he never did, especially not what happened next.

By early 1945 everyone knew the war was lost. The Red Army was advancing, and rumours spread of atrocities. In retaliation for the hardships inflicted by the Germans on the Russian population, the Red Army was ruthless in response. They raped and murdered; ransacked and destroyed.

The Nazi authorities had plans for an organised evacuation from Konigsberg, but it kept getting delayed and in panic and desperation, Simon's mother decided she could wait no longer. She bundled Simon's siblings into a hand-drawn cart along with all the blankets and food she could muster and with no warning, one cold winter's morning, they set off, walking west.

That was one of the things which had most annoyed Simon. He was never consulted. He liked to be in control of events. He liked to plan but his mother had always presented him with surprises.

They stuck to the main roads, heading for Berlin and soon met neighbours who were making the same journey. This small band of refugees became a caravan of chaos as they caught up with others fleeing for their lives at pinch points where vehicles had become stuck in the snow.

Simon did his best to help as he felt a heavy responsibility being the eldest child, but he was constantly cold and hungry. The wind cut through his clothing and chilled him to the bone and his boots wore out, so his feet were always sodden.

Black chopped a cherry tomato in two and popped one half in his mouth. He had never forgotten being hungry but strangely, his reaction to this was to eat sparingly. He carried no surplus fat on his body and every morsel he ate was taken slowly and carefully as a tribute to those times of hunger.

On that long march, aged twelve, death was all around him. Regularly, they had to dive into ditches to avoid being sprayed with bullets from low-flying aircraft and usually, some people didn't get up. Their route was littered with bodies that had succumbed to the cold, stress and starvation. They were rolled to the side of the road and the survivors carried on. However, if they found a horse's carcass, it was quickly butchered, and they would feast on the rancid meat.

One night they came across an abandoned bunker and took refuge inside. Black remembered with disbelief that this cold, concrete pit, dark and damp was actually a welcome relief from the wind-driven sleet that waited for them outside.

Suddenly there was shouting and shooting. The Red Army had arrived. They called all the women and children out of the bunker and made them line up at gunpoint while a guard stood at the entrance and told the men to stay put. Someone asked his age and his mother said he was nine. That lie showed she loved him, he thought, and he was so malnourished it was just about believable.

He could see it now. It was dark and trying to snow and he stood, shivering silently, wondering what would happen next and then he watched as the soldiers threw hand-grenades into the bunker. Black winced as he remembered the explosions and screams and then the groaning. The Red Army finished them off with their machine guns and then all was silent.

He knocked back the last of his sherry in one swig and wiped his mouth with a napkin.

In their case, the rumours had been exaggerated. There was no rape; just murder. The Red Army sent them on their way and with their heads hung low and little expectation of survival, miraculously, despite all the odds, they ended up in a Displaced Persons Camp in the British Zone of Berlin. Living space was cramped, food was in short supply and people continued to die as the relief of safety was overtaken by the disease and disorders, they had brought with them. For Simon and his family, though, at least the war was over.

Black pulled out another piece of paper from the moneybox and unfolded it twice. It was a visa.

One day he and his mother had been called into an Army Administrator's office at the Displaced Persons Camp. They stood before a severe-looking man seated behind a desk. His hair had thinned, and he had thick eyebrows over narrow calculating eyes. The eyes were cold and showed no empathy towards them. Another, younger man, whispered into his elder's ear.

"You're going on holiday to England," the stern-looking man said and then he signed their visa. The whole process took, perhaps, a minute during which time his mother said nothing.

Within the week, Simon found himself living in Scarborough with a childless couple who ran a fish and chip shop. The wife was kind but dim, and the husband, well, he fried fish. To this day, the smell of fried food made him wretch.

The *holiday* stretched from weeks to months and then from months to years. No one explained anything to him but, eventually, Simon learnt that his mother and siblings had emigrated to Australia. He had no idea why he wasn't with them except he was once told his mother had been *over-wrought*.

When Black was eighteen, he went to Exeter University

to read History and German and after graduation, he went to Australia to visit his family. He was full of hope, but his hopes were dashed. His mother had married a farmhand and his siblings were uneducated and disinterested. The gap between them had become too wide to bridge.

Black looked at the signature on the visa. The signature that had ripped him from his family; the signature that had changed his life; the signature that took just a moment's thought. The signature was just one word. That word was 'Granville'.

Chapter Fourteen

August 1987 – London

It was now Thursday 27 August and the intense heat and humidity of the last couple of weeks was fading as the days shortened and summer prepared to pass on the baton to autumn.

The train slowed as it approached Kings Cross with Ian still wondering how to say 'good-bye' to Sophie.

"I don't like it that you are seeing him at home," she said, breaking the silence. "It makes me think this is not official MI6 business, which is good and bad."

"What do you mean?" Ian asked. He was self-assured enough to believe he was not out of his depth and actually found the prospect of another meeting with Simon Black quite exciting. He realised Black could be manipulative, but the fact MI6 was sharing information with him was enticing and he was impressed by the way Black calmly analysed situations.

"It is good because it is not serious enough to be MI6 business and bad because then why is he interested?"

"Don't worry," Ian said, wanting to close down the

conversation. "This should be the last I have to do with him."

"I hope so," she replied.

They held hands as Ian walked Sophie to the correct platform to catch the express train to Heathrow and then he turned to face her and clasped his arms around her waist.

"I don't know when I will see you again?" She said.

"Soon; just let me sort this business out and then I will be in touch." He kissed her gently on the lips and waited for her to board the train.

"Be careful," she said as she turned away, her eyes filling with tears.

They waved as the train left the station and then Ian headed for the taxi rank. Sophie was fretting over whether the relationship could survive the distance between Munich and Harrogate, whereas Ian's mind was firmly fixed on his meeting later that afternoon.

Ian asked the taxi driver to drop him somewhere around The Langham Hotel and All Souls Church. Langham Place was just at the top of Regent Street which put Ian within walking distance of his intended destinations without having to pay the taxi while it was stuck in traffic.

Ian liked All Souls and thought if he belonged to a church, this would be where he wanted to worship. It was designed by John Nash and was built in sand-coloured stone quarried near Bath. The entrance was particularly impressive being circular in shape and consisting of a portico supported by Corinthian columns which themselves rested on a stone floor raised above the pavement level by a semi-circle of six steps. This elegance was then repeated in the spire which rose above the portico and was further complemented by the curvature of BBC Broadcasting House which sat adjacent to the church. It was a good place to meet and people watch as minor celebrities could regularly be seen crossing the road to relax in the famous cocktail bar of The Langham after finishing work at the BBC.

Ian walked down the top half of Regent Street, turned right down Conduit Street, looked at some shoes in a shop window and then went on to Savile Row.

Danny welcomed him as Ian entered the gentleman's club-like premises of Anderson & Sheppard.

"Hello Sir," he said, shaking Ian's hand. "Your coat and trousers are ready for you. I will just go and get them."

Ian thought it was funny that Danny insisted on referring to his new suit as coat and trousers. He was, of course, right because traditionally only a three-piece was considered a suit and tailors referred to the jacket as a coat as it was usually worn over a waistcoat. That made what most people thought of as a coat an overcoat! It was important to hold on to such traditions, Ian mused even if only to confuse the Americans!

Ian quickly tried on the new suit, which fitted perfectly.

Danny ran his hands over the shoulders and stood back to check the fit.

"Yes, I'm happy with that, Sir. I think it's good to go."

"Yes, I'm happy with that too, thank you, Danny."

"And you will see I have made a pen pocket on the right-hand side. It is just wide enough for a pen and I have strengthened the lining with a strip of canvass inside so it can support the weight."

"Thank you, Danny."

"Shall I put these in a suit bag for you, Sir?"

"Yes, please."

Danny hung the new suit on a wooden hanger, put a polythene cover over it and then placed it in a branded, brown cotton suit bag which folded in two with a pair of handles coming together at the top so it could be carried.

Ian thanked everyone for their help and headed towards the exit.

"Do you need a taxi, Sir?" Danny asked.

"No, thank you. I'm just walking up the road to meet a friend."

Throughout the whole process, there had never been any mention of money. Ian had been accepted as a client of Anderson & Sheppard several years ago and from then on, they would simply assume he would not ask for anything if he could not afford it. Likewise, Ian never asked for the price. To do so would be distasteful and he knew the cost of his last suit. This one would be a similar price adjusted for inflation. In a couple of months, Ian would receive an invoice, hand-written in black ink and unlike some of the aristocracy, he would pay it by return. That way he could always rely on a warm welcome.

It was after 2.00 PM and Ian hadn't had any lunch, but he wasn't really sure what he wanted or where to go. In any case, he had been invited to that strange Victorian ritual called afternoon tea which he thought was completely the wrong time of day to be eating anything, let alone cucumber sandwiches and fancy cakes. It was too late for lunch and too early for dinner, so as far as Ian was concerned, it was over-rated, but he was willing to follow protocol on this occasion.

Ian meandered up to Oxford Street, via Maddox Street and New Bond Street, looking in the windows of the shops and galleries along the way and from there he cut up James Street, crossed Wigmore Street and went on to Marylebone High Street via Mandeville Place and Thayer Street. Ian knew Marylebone High Street and liked all the traditional shops. There were lots of specialist, individual retailers and, of course, Daunt Books where he enjoyed browsing when he had the chance. The High Street was, however, as far as he had ever ventured into Marylebone so, looking at his map; he took a left down George Street before reaching Daunt Books, into the more residential areas.

It had taken Ian an hour to reach Montagu Square,

although he could have done it in half the time, but he was still ten minutes early, so he stood at the south end of the square and took in his surroundings. It was clearly an exclusive area with substantial properties overlooking the gardens and expensive cars parked along either side.

Ian waited until 3.30 PM, walked down the western side of the square, went up a couple of steps to a wide front door and rang the bell.

Simon Black came down the stairs to meet him. He opened the door and gave Ian a broad grin which was a rare thing for him to do.

"Come in," he said and then looking at Ian's suit bag with the name Anderson & Sheppard written in white, he continued, "you must be a man with money using a royal tailor."

"I was thinking the same thing about you," Ian replied as he admired the grandeur of the entrance hall.

Black led the way up a flight of broad, stone stairs to a door on the right which opened into his apartment. Ian followed him in, along a dark, narrow hallway into a fairly large sitting room, passing a small kitchen on the left.

"Have a seat," Black said indicating towards two chairs and a table by the bay window.

The furniture was mahogany, the floorboards were polished with a large Persian carpet occupying the centre of the room but the chairs and table in the bay window were behind the main seating area. Ian noticed a games table to his right and a set of chess pieces. It looked as though a game was unfinished.

"I see you like chess," Ian said.

"I do. It is a game of strategy. I don't like games of chance."

"It looks as though that game has been abandoned," Ian said, looking towards the games table.

"Not at all; I have a friend in Germany, and we write to each other once a week, specifying a move each time. It can take a year to reach a conclusion. I like playing the long game."

Black went into the kitchen and came back with a pot of tea and cakes. Ian was hungry because he hadn't stopped for anything, but he didn't like tea. He wasn't sure why because it didn't taste that bad but the whole making process and the smell and colour, he found completely off-putting. However, he didn't feel he could object, so he helped himself to some milk, added the tea and took one of the Teacup Fancies.

"Ah, I see you put the milk in first," Black said as if it was important.

Ian had no idea of the significance of this but replied that his parents had made it like that. Apparently, however, the tea should be put in first. Like so many things in Britain, it was a class thing. The well-to-do could afford china cups which could cope with the temperature of the hot tea whereas the working classes drank out of pot mugs so added the milk first to stop them from cracking. Inadvertently, in Black's eyes, Ian had just revealed his parents' ordinary backgrounds.

"I've done a little digging since we last met," Ian said.

"Successful, I hope?" Black interjected excitedly.

"Yes. I went to Harrogate library and discovered the date of Judith Granville's wedding. I was then able to find the address from the Electoral Roll of what is now her ex-husband and I went to visit him."

"You clever boy; what did he say?"

Most people would find being addressed in this manner rather condescending, but it was just Black's way. He was patronising and arrogant, but Ian could tell that Black liked him.

"Well, he confirmed that Judith was pregnant when they got married and that Manfred Fuchs was the father although she didn't tell him that until after the birth. Apparently, Fuchs wanted to start a new life with her in Argentina but not long after he suggested it, he was killed."

Black leant back in his chair.

"Argentina's full of Nazis," he said. Then he broke off a small piece of cake and chewed it pensively. Ian took a sip of tea and tried not to wince.

Black started drumming his fingers on the arm of his chair with his right hand.

"I was wondering about the tabloids, but I think we

will stick with the broadsheets. It looks more professional. I think a simple interview with the legal section of The Times along the lines of *lawyer uncovers mystery while administering estate.* We'll start low key and let the tabloids pick it up from there."

"It's not my intention to go to the Press," Ian said. "I just want to make an appointment to see Judith Granville, give her the watch and the wallet and then that should be the end of my involvement."

"It's not as simple as that. You've let the cat out of the bag. You can't put it back in again."

"It's not my cat."

Black leant forward and frowned at him.

"You're an officer of the Supreme Court of Justice. You have a duty to the Court to see that justice is done. These people were fascists. They lent money to the Nazi party. The current chairman is the son of an SS officer. The public has a right to know."

"In relation to matters in which I am involved, my duty to the Court is to uphold the rule of law and the administration of justice. It is not my duty to drag up dirt from the past, which in any case is not fully substantiated. My client gave me a task. Returning the watch and the wallet completes that task." Ian had been firm because he was rattled now. He didn't like Black twisting the truth to create a tenuous legal obligation.

Black sat back and studied Ian carefully.

"You realise this could be the making of you? You're a provincial lawyer. I think you're better than that. Just think what this case could do for your career. You would be famous, and you could use that moment in the spotlight to join a niche practice here in London. I'd help you. I've got some useful connections."

"If I go to the Press with this Granville's bank could be finished. I don't want my success to be based on someone else's misfortune."

"Oh, grow up! They are the authors of their own misfortune. You would just be."

Ian interrupted. "Taking advantage of it."

Black's jaw drooped and his mouth opened slightly. He supported his chin with his left thumb and pressed his forefinger against his lips.

"Well, if you don't have the stomach for it," he said, letting his words trail off at the end.

Ian broke a faint smile and snorted.

"To exercise courage, you have to believe in the cause. This is a cause I don't believe in." Ian was immovable and, in that moment, Black realised this. He stood up suddenly and his whole attitude changed.

"Well, thank you for coming."

Ian jumped up. "I'm sorry I can't help you," he said a little sheepishly.

"Don't worry; I usually get my own way in the end."

Ian walked past the games table towards the door.

"I hope you find a winning move," he said, looking at the chess pieces.

Black was in an arrogant mode now. The charm was gone, and the icy exterior had returned.

"The secret to winning at chess is to force your opponent into making a fatal error," he said speaking as though he was a Grandmaster. He then grabbed a knight by the head and moved it two squares forward and one square to the right.

Ian glanced back. The knight was now vulnerable to being taken by his opponent's rook.

"Are you sure you want to do that? He asked.

Black dismissed the question with a wave of his hand.

"Sometimes, you have to sacrifice a knight to corner the king."

Chapter Fifteen

August 1987 – London

The next morning Simon Black arrived at work early, looking tired but freshly shaved with his hair washed and brushed and his cheeks revealing a slightly flushed complexion. He addressed Jane as he breezed past reception.

"Good morning, Jane. Ask the two Toms to come and see me when they get in, please."

"Yes, Sir," Jane replied, although Black hadn't waited for a response.

Twenty minutes later, there was a tap on Black's door and Tom Hatchet walked in with Tom Meeks just behind him.

"You wanted to see us?"

"Yes, come in gentlemen, have a seat." They pulled a couple of chairs up to his desk.

"You remember that Sutherland chap you picked up from the airport last week?"

Both Toms nodded in affirmation.

"Well, we have a bit of a problem. He came to see me

yesterday. Out of courtesy, I suppose, but it turns out he's a bit of a sleuth."

"How do you mean?" Hatchett asked.

"Before the start of the Second World War," Meeks slumped back in his chair but didn't dare roll his eyes. Here we go, he thought, the boring old fart is going to give us the long version. Black continued, "our Agent in Munich alerted us to the fact that a young banker with the name of Manfred Fuchs was making regular trips to London. He was a member of the Nazi party and later joined the SS. We tracked him here, in London and discovered he was frequenting with Lord Granville of Granville's bank," he paused for a reaction but both listeners looked blank.

"We came to the conclusion that Granville's bank was lending the Nazi party money and that Lord Granville was a fascist and a Nazi sympathiser although we never investigated him because that would be a matter for MI5. Fuchs was the focus of our attention."

"Quite so," Meeks said, looking through the window towards the Thames.

"Anyway, the War broke out, the relationship came to an end, and Fuchs was killed by a sniper's bullet."

"Ouch," Meeks said. Black wasn't sure if he was adding the sound effects just to annoy him or if he was expressing empathy for Fuchs.

"So, the file was simply archived until a couple of weeks ago when one of our associates in Munich, Frau

Eschenbach, alerted us to the fact that Sutherland was on location and asking questions."

Tom Hatchett screwed up his eyes and wrinkled his brow.

"What sort of questions?"

"Questions about Manfred Fuchs. His background and career; surviving relatives. That sort of thing."

"Sounds a bit bazaar to me," Meeks interjected.

"Wait for it," Black said like a comedian about to deliver a punch line.

"I don't care if you call it coincidence or destiny but Sutherland, he's a solicitor by the way, did a Will for an ex-soldier who only turns out to be the sniper who shot Fuchs in The Ardennes in 1945."

"Small world," Meeks said sardonically.

"But why the questions? Hatchett pressed, "and why go to Munich?"

"Apparently, Field, that's the name of the sniper, took some of Fuchs's personal belongings from his corpse, and he wanted Sutherland to return them to his family. Pang of conscience on his death bed I suspect."

Black was animated and revelling in the telling of his story.

"So, why is that a problem for us?" Hatchett asked, which showed at least one of them was following the storyline.

"It isn't; but during his digging, he discovered that

Manfred Fuchs was the father of Frederick Granville, the current chairman of Granville's bank." Black finished his sentence with a loud *ha* and waited for the reply. Both Hatchett and Meeks were watching him intently but didn't say anything. Black sat back and calmed himself.

"Anyway, Sutherland came to see me yesterday and said he was going to the Press. I tried to dissuade him, but he thinks it's his moral duty; the public has a right to know and all that crap."

Meeks suddenly became engaged and shifted his chair diagonally towards Hatchett and Black.

"Will the Press be interested in the fact that forty-odd years ago, Frederick Granville was fathered by an SS officer?"

"They will if they're also told Granville's bank was financing the Nazi party and that's how the whole relationship started."

"Does Sutherland know that?" Meeks asked.

"Yes."

"How?" Meeks persisted.

"I don't know," Black said, dropping his right hand into the pocket of his jacket and jingling the keys to his apartment. "The point is he is going to the Press, and he's going to tell them everything. Now we don't know what their reaction will be or how the public will react, but it could be a disaster. If the story really grabs people's imagination, it could even cause a run on the bank, and there hasn't been one of those since 1866 when Overend, Gurney and Co lost all their money on railway stocks."

"I still can't see what it has to do with us," Hatchett said, "it is more MI5 than MI6."

"It isn't MI5 or MI6 really. However, I think the least we can do is warn them. Just give them the heads-up so they can get their PR advisors thinking about how they want to react and give them the chance to raise their liquidity if they need to."

Hatchett and Meeks nodded in agreement.

"What I want you to do is go to see Frederick Granville and just say we are aware of this and thought you ought to know in case you want to take any evasive action; that's all."

The two Toms murmured in acceptance and stood up to leave Black's office and Black walked over to his office window. Meeks shut the door behind him and turned to Hatchett.

"Do you believe all that?"

"Why shouldn't I?"

"He rattled his keys."

"What do you mean?"

"He rattled his keys. That's his *tell*. When he rattles his keys, you know he's lying or nervous about something."

"I don't see how he could make up something like that."

"No, but he's holding something back. I don't think

that was the full story."

"Well, I'm going back in anyway. There is something else I'm concerned about."

Meeks walked down the corridor and Hatchett turned back and knocked on the door.

"Come in."

Black was staring out of the window.

"I'm sorry to bother you again; it's just that I'm concerned that by speaking with Frederick Granville, we will be acting beyond our authority. Wouldn't we be leaking information confidential to MI6 and revealing our hand, so to speak? I mean, Granville's bank won't know we have anything on them."

"Ah, you think we will be acting ultra vires?" Black said, turning towards him.

"Well, I think we might be."

Black moved a little closer.

"I'm fifty-five next year and I don't want to do this job forever. I certainly want to retire before I'm sixty; travel a bit, watch the cricket, have time to read. And I think you're the man to replace me. Meeks certainly isn't up to it. But you have to be able to make the difficult decisions if necessary and look at the bigger picture. What do you think the Bank of England would say if there was a run on Granville's bank and they found out we had sat on sensitive information?"

"Well, when you put it like that."

"Exactly, it's a matter of national interest. Now knuckle down and let me know how you get on. It might come as a bit of a shock if Frederick Granville doesn't know who his real father is."

Black went back to the window and gazed out across the Thames. He had made his move. The next move was up to the Granvilles. If he had judged them correctly, they would do something rash. He hoped he hadn't put Ian in danger; he liked him but the Granvilles would surely try to shut him up? One way or another, he would get the information out. The important thing was it would appear he had clean hands. He chuckled to himself. The sky was about to fall in on the Granvilles and they had no idea he even existed.

Meeks took some lasagne and chips from the hotplate, put them on his tray and sought out Hatchett, who was sat eating a sandwich in the staff canteen.

"Are you ready? We might as well go and see him after lunch."

Hatchett put his head in his hands and tugged at his hair.

"Oh, I'm dreading this. We're about to tell Frederick Granville his father was in the SS and his bank is about to collapse. Aren't you bothered?"

"No, I just think about my pocket. If it's good for my career, I don't care."

Frederick Granville was also eating lunch, at a pub in

Shepherd Market, just off Curzon Street. He had chosen sautéed chicken liver and apple salad, which he was washing down with a glass of Beaujolais. He mopped up the meat juices with some French bread and got up to leave.

A waitress hastened towards his table, but he just took a couple of notes from his money clip and threw them on his side plate. There was just enough to cover the cost of the meal and leave a small tip.

He walked outside into the Georgian Square and looked around to check he didn't recognise anyone. He loathed what he was about to do next but what was a divorced man of forty-seven meant to do? It had become far too risky to use the secretaries and, in any case, they couldn't cope with his predilections.

He walked around the corner, down a narrow alley, opened a side door and then bolted up some stairs to where a madame sat behind a desk. He was wearing an immaculate grey suit with a white shirt and a pink and grey striped tie. He could smell stale smoke and he baulked at the thought of it clinging to his clothes.

The madame eyed him up. He was not unattractive. He was of medium height and slim with cropped grey hair, although his dark brown eyes were small and too close together and the peaked eyebrows over them looked a bit odd.

A man like that shouldn't find it too hard to attract a

woman but she realised it was his particular tastes that were the difficulty.

He threw the cash down on the table. It was more than the going rate as this establishment specialised.

"Just through there, please. Someone will be with you shortly."

Frederick Granville went into a dingy bedroom with a wrought iron bed. There was a dressing table and chair opposite the foot of the bed. He took off his jacket, placed it over the chair and then moved the chair to one side.

A young Thai woman entered the room dressed in a French maid's outfit, put her hands in the prayer position and bowed her head.

"Hello Sir, my name is Lamai."

Frederick Granville looked her up and down. She had long straight hair almost to her waist, but it was dyed blonde, which looked a bit unusual against her darker skin. She was shorter than he liked but this was compensated by the fact that she was wearing some very high-heeled, black stilettos.

"Turn around and put your hands on the dressing table." Lamai did as she was told.

"Bend over." Lamai had been warned that he would want to smack her, but the madame had said she was right outside the door if needed and it was only play-acting.

Frederick Granville lifted the cheap, black satin hem of the dress over her back and pulled down her knickers to reveal her bare bottom. He then ripped the black leather belt from his trousers with such speed it made a cracking noise which he found arousing. Then he whipped her with the belt across the buttocks. First one side, then the other. She gasped at the sting. This was much harder than she had been expecting. Six times he did it, leaving her bottom bright red as the blood rushed to the surface of the skin. He then put his hand under her hair just behind the nape of her neck, twisted the hair over and held it in his clenched fist like a set of reins on a horse. He pulled her hair and her head cocked back towards him. She was finding it hard to breathe and then; he penetrated her.

Thankfully, it was over quickly. Lamai pulled up her knickers, straightened herself and turned to face him. A single tear was rolling down her left cheek. Frederick looked at it and slapped her across the face.

"Get out," he said.

Lamai would not see much of the cash he had thrown down at the madame, but some would be sent home to Bangkok, where she had a child being brought up by her mother and an extended family to support. She had come to London on the promise of being found a rich husband; that was never the intention of the Agency that enticed her.

When Frederick Granville arrived back at the bank, the two Toms were waiting for him. He was not in a good mood. He felt dirty and wanted a shower. Normally, he would have refused to see unexpected visitors, but with MI6, he assumed he had no choice.

He took them into an upstairs meeting room, next to his office.

"What is it you want?" He said tetchily.

"Well, it's rather delicate, really," Hatchett started.

"Oh, get on with it. I haven't got all day."

Hatchett's sympathy was rapidly vanishing, so he decided to be brief and to the point.

"Just before the War, MI6 received information regarding a relationship between your bank and a certain Manfred Fuchs who was a German national and a member of the Nazi party. He later joined the SS."

"So, that's not illegal," Frederick snapped.

"It was thought, at the time, that your bank was lending money to the Nazis and they became an enemy of the State."

Frederick took a deep breath.

"You're viewing things with hindsight. My understanding is we didn't break any rules at the time. Anyway, you will have difficulty trying to prove it."

Meeks interrupted. "We're not here to criticise you. We're here to warn you."

"Warn me! About what?"

"About a young lawyer called Ian Sutherland. Manfred Fuchs was shot by a sniper towards the end of the War and recently the sniper instructed Sutherland to prepare a Will for him."

"I don't follow," Frederick said, the side of his mouth twitching.

"Sutherland was tasked, by the now-deceased sniper, to return some personal items belonging to Manfred Fuchs and so he travelled to Munich where he traced Manfred's sister. This led to his discovery of the relationship between Fuchs and your family."

Meeks paused while Frederick dabbed the sweat from his forehead.

"There's something else," Meeks spoke slowly. "We believe Manfred Fuchs was your father."

"Well, I knew it wasn't that sop David Moor," Frederick barked. "Is that it? Is that all you've come to tell me?"

This wasn't the reaction they had been expecting.

"There is one more thing," Hatchett said. "We understand Sutherland may be going to the Press with his story. He wants to gain a bit of fame and fortune, apparently. We don't know how it will play out, but it was thought you should be informed because forewarned is forearmed as they say." As Hatchett relayed these words, he had a strange feeling that he wasn't sure he really believed them.

"Yes, quite right. Well, thank you for coming. I'm sure we can deal with it." Frederick stood up and opened the door. "My secretary will see you out."

The two Toms left the room and Frederick shut the door

behind them. He paced around for a minute and looked at his watch. He knew what he had to do. He would do what he always did in times of trouble. He would go to his grandfather. He picked up the phone to his secretary.

"I'm going to Florin Hall. Get me a taxi. If I can make the three-thirty train, I should get to York around five-thirty. Get one of the staff to pick me up at the station. We should get back to Florin Hall for six-thirty."

"Yes, sir," she replied.

Ian had been feeling flat all day. It was the end of his holiday, he was missing Sophie, and the meeting with Simon Black had been a bit of an anti-climax. He felt he was right not to go to the Press, but he was now no longer in the loop. However, he had just one last task to complete and he steeled himself to get on with it.

Judith Granville accepted his telephone call and when he explained that he had some items belonging to Manfred to give to her, she agreed to see him.

"You can come today for a drink before dinner," she said. "The Stables are just to the right of Florin Hall. Come about six-thirty."

Chapter Sixteen

August 1987 – North Yorkshire

Ian found that if he was feeling a little low, the best thing to do was take some exercise, so he decided to go on a run. He went straight from his flat into Valley Gardens and then up through the pinewoods. From there he ran down Otley Road and right around The Stray before returning home for a shower.

It was an easy run through what his housemaster used to call *the fleshpots of Yorkshire*. Not like the Wilson Run. Ian thought about that as he paced the flatlands of central Harrogate. The race always started too quickly as one hundred boys from the upper and lower sixth set off from Sedbergh town centre for the Howgill Fells. By the time they reached them and left the road they had spread out and they had to dig deep as they started the ascent. The Howgill Fells were okay. Well grazed and firm underfoot but the runners soon had to come off the hillside, cross the road and climb the marshy bogs of Baugh Fell. This was riddled with streams and in March they were swollen by rain and snowmelt. The runners waded across the most violent of these clinging on to a rope and then had to climb a steep bank called Muddy Slide. This is where the wind joined in to play and froze the runners who were usually soaked to the waist. The tufts of coarse grass turned many an ankle and when Ian came off the fell at Danny Bridge, he turned around and cursed it.

The run back to town from there was all on the road and downhill and it was almost a luxury for the runners as they made a last effort to secure their finishing positions in the annals of school history.

In more recent times the race had been called barbaric and there had been calls to make it easier and change the time of year, but the alumni were its strongest defenders. It was character building and having run the race, life's other obstacles seemed somehow less difficult.

Ian showered, shaved and put on his new suit. He thought he better look his best if he was visiting Florin Hall and it would soon be autumn and inappropriate to wear a lightweight suit. He wore it with a light blue shirt and a chocolate and blue patterned tie, all of which made him look rather dashing.

He put Manfred's watch and wallet in a small bag he had saved from his last trip to Turnbull & Asser and seeing the spy pen on his side table, he grabbed that at the last minute too. It felt right to take something of John Field's with him. John Field had started this adventure and although he couldn't be there for the finish, the pen, somehow, maintained the connection.

Florin Hall lay in the centre of a triangle somewhere between Ripon, Harrogate and Boroughbridge. Set in two thousand acres, it was not easy to get to because it was not part of a village community but a self-contained estate off the beaten track.

Ian passed a row of terraced cottages, historically occupied by agricultural workers, then found the main entrance to the Hall. There were two stone pillars with an animal's head mounted on each. The stone was badly worn, though, and Ian couldn't tell if they were lions, eagles, or, perhaps, griffins. Between the stone pillars were large wrought iron gates that were open. On either side of these was a small gatehouse.

Ian let the Jag purr gently up the driveway as the rain went pitter-pat on its canvas roof. The drive was straight with flat parkland on either side, a few grazing sheep and some specimen trees but no signs of the Hall itself. Ian checked the mileage on his speedometer and noted that this vista remained unchanged for half a mile. The drive then took a sharp left and there, a further two-tenths of a mile ahead, Ian could see the outline of the property. He approached slowly, the outline becoming more dominant on the horizon as he did so and then he saw it in all its glory. It looked magnificent. Built in the early 18th century and designed with the help of Sir Christopher Wren, the house fitted perfectly into its surroundings. It was constructed from a soft pink brick with three layers of beautifully proportioned Georgian windows.

The drive then forked, offering the choice of turning right or continuing straight on to the Hall which was set behind a further set of stone pillars, wrought iron railings and hedging so Ian took the first option although there was no sign of The Stables.

Around the corner, they appeared. They sat directly in line with the Hall but discretely hidden by trees and hedges.

The Stables were Grade 1 listed and the frontage was built of stone with an archway in the centre. They looked too big to be one residence and Ian wasn't sure where to go so he parked outside beside some other vehicles and then walked through the archway. He opened his eyes wide in amazement as the archway led into a courtyard with three sides of two-storey red brick buildings lining the remaining boundaries.

You could tell they had been stables because while the windows in the upper storey were of normal size, the ground floor windows were arched and had clearly been used as entrances in the past. Right in front of him, in the centre of the property forming the back of the courtyard, was a large double doorway with a solid oak door and a large knocker so Ian approached and gave it two loud bangs.

Judith Granville opened the door. She had short hair

which had obviously gone grey and then been dyed blonde. She was of medium height with a full but not too over-weight figure. She was wearing a tweed skirt just below the knee which exuded quality, a turtle-neck cashmere sweater and a string of pearls.

"Mr Sutherland, I presume?"

"Yes, how do you do?"

"Come in. Would you like a drink? I'm having a gin and tonic."

"Thank you. That sounds lovely but just a splash of gin please, as I'm driving."

"This way."

Judith led Ian into a sitting room overlooking the rear garden. Everything was beautifully appointed, but Ian didn't want to appear rude, so he maintained his focus on Judith although he did notice a silver-framed photograph of a young man in pride of place on a grand piano.

"Thank you for seeing me."

"Well, it all sounds very intriguing." Judith had taken two glasses from a cocktail cabinet, dropped in some ice and lemon and more than a splash of gin.

"Oh, dear. There's no tonic left. Just a moment." She picked up the telephone and rang the Hall.

"Sinclair, I've run out of tonic. Bring some over, will you? I'm entertaining a Mr Sutherland who is a solicitor from Ryders in Harrogate."

Ian did not realise but this rather full description was

an elaborate code between mistress and servant to indicate the level of trappings to be applied. Sinclair would not arrive with a bottle of Schweppes but rather a cocktail shaker filled with ice and tonic delivered on a silver tray.

"Is this Frederick?" Ian asked, picking up the photograph and thinking to himself that there was a clear resemblance to the photograph of Manfred in the wallet.

"Yes, it is," Judith said a little surprised at his familiarity. "Now do have a seat; Sinclair will be with us shortly." She took a deep breath.

So, what's this all about? You said you had some items belonging to Manfred Fuchs."

"It's a little sensitive, I'm afraid," Ian said gently. "I was instructed to draw up a Will for a man called John Field. He made his Will last March and died shortly afterwards. He was a sniper during the Second World War." Ian looked down. "He gave me these and asked me to pass them on to Manfred's family."

Ian gave her the bag containing the watch and wallet. Judith looked inside and pulled out the wallet. She turned it over in her hands several times without opening it, at which point Sinclair knocked at the door and walked in.

"Your tonic, my lady."

Judith ignored him for a second and then distractedly told him to fill the glasses. He did so, handed her a drink and then gave the second glass to Ian.

"That will be all – thank you," she said curtly.

Judith opened the wallet and took out the ID card that bore Manfred's photograph. She looked sad but her eyes were dry. She then brought it to her lips and kissed it.

"I loved him; you know."

"I'm sure," Ian said softly.

"He was the only man I ever met who could stand up to my father. He engaged with him on equal terms. I know the SS did bad things, but when I met him, before the War, he was handsome and decisive. He knew exactly what he wanted, and I admired that."

"I understand," Ian said this with some sensitivity. Judith looked at him carefully and decided she liked him.

"How did you make the connection with me?"

"I went to the address on the ID card and met Manfred's sister. She indicated that you were the person in the picture, and she thought it was more appropriate for you to have the items."

Judith nodded. "Gertrud, isn't it?"

"Yes."

"I haven't seen her in years. In fact, I think I only met her once."

She picked up the watch and checked the inscription.

"I remember buying him this. He was absolutely thrilled," she paused. "Thank you for bringing me these."

"It's my pleasure. It squares the circle so to speak."

"Yes, it does."

Ian finished his drink and stood up to go.

"We were going to make a new life together, you know, after the War, in Argentina. Then he got killed. Do you know how he was killed?"

"I believe he was stranded behind Allied lines in the Ardennes where he was shot. It would have been instant."

"Yes, well, thank you for coming," Judith said hurriedly as she escorted Ian to the front door. There was a sombre quietness between them when she suddenly broke the silence.

"There wasn't anything suspicious about his death was there?"

Ian smiled kindly. "Not that I'm aware of. John Field was concerned that the intelligence was inaccurate regarding the number of soldiers stranded with Manfred and I understand your father took an interest in Manfred's career, but that was only natural, I suppose, given the family connection."

"It's just he died so soon after writing to me with his plans for Argentina."

Ian didn't say anything but continued walking to the door.

"Well, thank you for having me."

"No, thank you for coming."

"Goodbye."

"Goodbye."

While Ian had been talking to Judith, Frederick had been talking to his grandfather.

The gardener, who doubled up as a chauffeur when needed, had collected Frederick from York station in Lord Granville's old Mercedes-Benz 450 SEL 6.9. Lord Granville was ninety-three years old. If he drove at all, it was only around the estate, so he had never bothered replacing the Mercedes which still had low mileage.

On arrival, Frederick had brushed past Lord Granville's fourth wife, who was a sprightly, smartly dressed, trim lady of similar age to Frederick's mother and gone straight into his grandfather's study.

The old man was sat in his leather chair, looking out over his estate. He had red, watery eyes and a hunched posture but his mind was alert and he still retained his vicious tongue.

"Hello, grandfather."

"What do you want? You look all hot and bothered."

"I've had a visit from MI6 today."

"Why, what have you done?"

"I haven't done anything, but they know we financed the Nazis before the War, and they know Manfred Fuchs was my father."

"How the devil do they know that?"

"Some lawyer called Sutherland has been fishing, apparently, and he's about to tell the whole story to the Press."

"What!"

Lord Granville grabbed his glass of malt whiskey and

took a swig. He had a glass on the go all day and called it his medicine because "it thinned the blood and was better than taking warfarin."

"The lawyer acted for the bastard who shot my father; that's how it's all come about."

"Well, you'll have to stop him. He could ruin us."

"How?"

Lord Granville had stood up and was facing Frederick but kept one hand on the side of the winged-back chair for support.

"What did you think when you came up the drive?"

"Pardon?" Frederick had no idea what his grandfather meant.

"What did you think when you came up the drive?"

"I didn't think anything."

Lord Granville finished his last dreg of whiskey and shouted for Sinclair.

"Sinclair; more medicine."

He turned and looked out over the estate.

"My father bought this estate off an idiot who couldn't afford to pay his gambling debts. His family had designed it and put in all the effort for over two hundred years. The idiot lost the lot in the twinkling of an eye. We got it because we were his bankers, and I'm not about to lose it – ever." Frederick could see the sheer determination on his face as his grandfather continued.

"When I come up the drive, I look around and I realise

I love this place more than anything else. If this gets out there could be a run on the bank and if that happened, we could lose everything, and I mean everything." He turned to face Frederick and looked him in the eye.

"You will just have to do whatever it takes to stop this lawyer from blabbing to the Press," he said, emphasizing the word "whatever."

Sinclair entered with a fresh glass of Malt whiskey.

"Your medicine Sir."

"Ask Judith to come over, will you? I need to speak to her." Lord Granville snapped.

"I believe she is engaged with a lawyer from Ryders called Mr Sutherland, although, excuse me," Sinclair moved to the window, "I do believe he is just leaving."

Frederick looked at his grandfather in disbelief and ran to the window to see the E-type Jaguar pulling away.

"What does he want?"

"What they always want. Money!" The old man shouted. "He's probably asking for hush money."

"Sinclair get me the keys to the Mercedes. I'm going after him."

Frederick ran down the steps of the entrance to the Hall as his mother approached to see her father. They were too far apart to say anything to each other, but Judith could see he looked as fired up as she felt, and she suspected the reason was the same as usual – Lord Granville.

Judith marched into his study.

"You had him killed, didn't you?"

"What?" Granville barked.

"Manfred; you had him killed."

"Don't be ridiculous! I suppose that lawyer has put that stupid idea in your head."

"Not at all, but it's a bit of a coincidence that just after I receive a letter suggesting we start afresh in Argentina, he gets shot."

"I'm powerful, but I'm not that powerful," Granville growled.

"I want to know; did you have anything to do with his death?" Judith shouted.

"Do you really want to know? Really?" He said angrily.

"Yes."

"The silly idiot gave his position away. Belgian partisans had alerted us to the situation, then he revealed his identity. I just suggested we sent in the snipers. We needed a bit of success given that the Battle of the Bulge had largely been an American show. Anyway, he was holding hostages."

"So, you had him killed?"

"We were just following protocol," Lord Granville hesitated. "I might have reduced the numbers given to us by the partisans, that's all."

"That's all!" Judith screamed at him. "You knew he would be shot."

"I did what I had to for the sake of the family. Just like

Frederick is doing now."

"What do you mean?" Judith's expression had changed from anger to concern.

"Well, he's gone after that lawyer before he goes to the Press."

"He's not going to the Press. He just wanted to give me back some of Manfred's personal belongings," Judith said with exasperation.

"Oh, dear," Lord Granville said coldly. "That's not what Frederick thinks."

Chapter Seventeen

August 1987 – North Yorkshire

The light rain of earlier in the day had turned into an August downpour so Ian ran to the Jag thankful that he had already put up the hood.

Florin Hall had a separate entrance and exit, so Ian took a left out of the Stables parking area and then followed a much shorter route to a more modest set of gates with just one gatehouse where the drive re-joined the main road approximately a mile nearer Ripon than the entrance.

The rain was thick and heavy, bouncing back off the road so Ian took it slowly not realising that Frederick was racing up behind him.

With the daylight fading quickly, hastened by the darkening clouds, Ian followed the Boroughbridge Road towards the outskirts of Ripon. Traffic was light, headlights and wipers were on, but Ian was in no rush as he made his way back to Harrogate relieved, or so he thought, that this whole saga was over. He started daydreaming, thinking about Sophie, when he noticed a gold-coloured Mercedes overtaking vehicles behind him, weaving in and out of the traffic rather precariously.

Frederick hadn't really got a plan. He knew the family and their whole way of life was in jeopardy and he believed it was his duty to eliminate the threat. Quite how he hadn't decided but he saw Ian as the source of the problem.

Ian had taken a back road past some council houses on the outskirts of Ripon to save going into the town itself and as the area was built up it was not until Ian reached the A61 to Harrogate that the Mercedes actually came up behind him. Ian was approaching a series of S bends known locally as the daffodil bends, as the embankments either side of the road had been planted with thousands of daffodil bulbs, when he saw the Mercedes right on his tail. He had no idea who was driving the Mercedes. He just thought it was too close and wanted to get away, so he put his foot down.

After bearing right, the road took a sharp left, then a sharp right, followed by a long left and a sharp right. Ian took these corners at about 55 mph, which was about the safe driving limit, especially in heavy rain. There was then a short straight and looking in his driver's mirror he saw the Mercedes still on his tail with its headlights full on. It was getting dangerously close. Ian couldn't see the driver because the plastic rear window in the hood of the Jag was steamed up. He thought that it was just some idiot, so he speeded up to get away from him.

Ian went through another series of bends taking a sharp

right and a sharp left at just over 60mph. The rear wheels of the Jag started to slip as he made it to another straight stretch about four-tenths of a mile in length with woodland trees on the left-hand side and an isolated pair of cottages on the right. The Mercedes was still with him, so Ian accelerated to 80 mph. It was then he noticed the number plate, which was JG 1 and managed to get a glimpse of the driver. He saw just enough to realise that the driver was the same person whose photograph was sitting on the grand piano in Judith Granville's sitting room. Suddenly he realised; Frederick Granville was following him.

"What does he want?" Ian said to himself. He thought about stopping but it was heaving down with rain, so he pressed on. The road took a sharp right, followed by a sharp left and the Jag was now at the limit of its road-holding abilities. It just clung on as Ian gripped the wooden steering wheel for all his might. Ahead was a long straight stretch, bounded by open fields, known as the five-furlong straight and Ian pressed his foot flat to the floor. Water was spraying everywhere as his speed approached 100 mph. Ian looked in his mirror, but the Mercedes was still right behind him, its 6.9-litre engine effortlessly matching the 3.8 litres of the lighter, more agile Jag.

Ian braked hard as he approached the end of the straight and took a sharp right at the top of a hill leading down to the hamlet of Wormald Green. The tail of the Jag flipped out and he just managed to apply enough opposite lock without going off the road as he headed down the hill. He was hoping that the Mercedes wouldn't make it, but it was a late seventies creation and had the benefit of anti-lock brakes and hydropneumatic self-levelling suspension which helped the road holding and neither of which featured in an E-type Jag from the early sixties.

Going down the hill, Frederick was right behind him and as Ian tried to negotiate the sharp bend to the left, Frederick nudged the back nearside corner of the Jag just as the rear wheels were slipping at the apex of the corner. Suddenly, Ian's perception of the situation changed. Up to now, he thought the car chase was just boyish high spirits but now he realised this was something far more sinister and he was worried.

"Is he mad?" Ian said out loud.

The back end of the Jag spun out across the road and within seconds, as Ian frantically turned the steering wheel to the right, he found himself travelling along the grass verge in the direction of Harrogate. Ian was breaking, skidding and fighting to stabilise the car while the Mercedes shot passed him as it was still on the road. Momentarily, Ian saw Frederick's face turn towards him, and he was laughing.

In front of Ian was a bus shelter but something else must have hit it previously because it consisted of a pile of bricks and rubble on top of which was placed its flat sheet roof. It formed a ramp and with that feeling of dread you get just before a car crash; Ian pictured the Jag flying through the air unless he did something quickly. He pulled down hard right on the steering wheel and the Jag responded, its front wheels catching the tarmac of the road and then, gaining traction, pulling the rest of the car with it. However, the back end was still spinning so the Jag turned through 180 degrees, all the time Ian braking and fighting to bring it into a straight line.

Now Ian was travelling back towards Ripon, with the Mercedes going in the opposite direction towards Harrogate except that Ian hadn't quite made a 180-degree turn. The Jag was pointing slightly towards the grass verge on Ian's left where the upcoming corner was marked with black and white plastic posts about four feet in height with red reflector lights on the top section. Despite his best efforts to stop, Ian hit one with his front nearside wheel. The Jag seemed to drive up it, the post bent in two and then, at last, the Jag came to a stop at the side of the road facing Ripon.

Frederick had been watching in his driver's mirror in disbelief as he expected Ian to fly into the field to the left of the bus shelter. Quickly, he commenced a three-point turn as Ian slumped back in the driver's seat and sighed with relief.

I'm okay, Ian thought even though he had carried out a driving manoeuvre far beyond his desire or expertise.

Smoke or steam started hissing out of the Jag's engine

and Ian thought he'd better get out quickly even though it was still pouring with rain.

Frederick was sat in the stationary Mercedes perhaps a hundred yards or so behind the Jag and seeing the opportunity decided it was too good to let pass. He pressed the accelerator to the floor, causing the wheels of the Mercedes to spin as it lurched forward. Ian was unaware of what was happening. He was presenting a side-on profile for Frederick and was still shutting the driver's door of the Jag. A split second beforehand, he may have heard something or seen the car coming out of the corner of his eye, but he had no time to react. The Mercedes struck him on the left thigh, sending him flying through the air.

Ian remembered the force of the push. It was unlike anything he had ever experienced before. So powerful, he was thrown forward and above the Mercedes which came to a halt in front of him.

Ian landed on his left hand and right ankle. He felt the flesh of his hand tare as it scraped the tarmac and his ankle buckle and snap under the force of the impact. Then the rest of his body came thumping to the ground. He could feel blood trickling down his hand, and he was soaking wet. Instinctively, he sat up and shuffled backwards off the road. He felt the water seep through to his underpants as his backside made contact with the sodden ground of the grass verge and then, horrified, he realised he was blind.

"I can't see. I can't see," he shouted in panic, hoping a passer-by had stopped at the scene of the accident but the only response was the sound of laughing as Frederick walked towards him.

"Well how very convenient for me, Mr Sutherland." Frederick's voice was chilled with evil intent. "Now, I am going to have to pull you back to the road so I can reverse over you. I need to make this look like an accident."

Ian couldn't believe how quickly this had all gone so badly wrong when suddenly, Ian's vision was filled with a big, circular red light; like a burning sun, blurred at the edges. Quickly, the image started to sharpen and then divide in two as Ian's eyes focussed and he realised he was looking at the rear lights of the Mercedes.

I must have gone blind with shock, Ian thought with massive relief that his sight had been restored.

Frederick grabbed Ian by his right ankle and started to drag him towards the road, still thinking he was blind. Ian tried to kick him away and winced as the pain shot up his leg. He hadn't fully assessed his injuries. His right ankle was so painful it must be broken and his whole left leg felt as though it was going to burst. His suit trousers were torn where the Mercedes had hit him, probably because his leg had smashed the headlight, and there was a small circular cut bleeding steadily.

Ian had slithered on to his stomach and was pulling himself back up the grass verge, his fingers clawing into the wet mud. Frederick came back at him and flung himself over Ian's legs realising he had to incapacitate him before dragging him back to the road. He saw the cut on Ian's thigh and the started thumping it over and over again. Ian was still on his stomach and groaned with pain but rather than trying to fight Frederick off he fumbled for the pen in his jacket pocket. He got it out, but his fingers were caked with mud and he dropped it as Frederick started pulling him back towards the road. Ian slid over on to his back and Frederick moved his position so that he was now sitting on Ian's pelvis. Frederick hit Ian across the side of his face. Ian felt the bone of Frederick's fist smash against the bone of his jaw as his face was flung into the mud. Frederick was sat over him now and was clearly just going to punch him from side to side. Ian lifted his arm and hit Frederick back but there was no power in the punch. It was as though Ian was fighting underwater and he could not understand what had happened to his strength. Waves of pain kept flowing through him; the adrenalin holding back the shock.

Frederick struck Ian again, this time on the other side of his face and as Ian's head was thrust to the side, his eyes started to roll. He willed himself to remain conscious and grabbing hold of Frederick's tie pulled himself up so that they were looking at each other with their noses only an inch apart. Ian had no idea why Frederick had attacked him, but he knew his life was in danger. In a desperate attempt to save himself, Ian bit that soft piece of flesh on the bottom of Frederick's chin and held on like a terrier. Frederick screamed and sat back, trying to push Ian off, but Ian clenched his teeth with every ounce of strength he had left. Eventually, the flesh tore and Ian's hold broke. Frederick fell back blood pouring from his face.

Ian swivelled back on to his stomach and grasped the pen. Quickly he undid the top and held the butt of the pen in his right palm with the blade pointing upwards and resting tight against his forearm. Frederick dived on him again and pulled Ian over on to his back. He gripped Ian around the neck and started to strangle him. Ian flipped the pen over and with one final effort thrust it under Frederick's jaw. The blade sliced through the soft flesh behind his chin, went straight through his tongue and pinned it to the roof of his mouth. Blood and saliva spurted out of Frederick's mouth as though he was blowing bubbles and then he fell back choking. He staggered to his feet, blood still squirting out of the sides of his mouth, the stiletto acting as a staple holding the centre together. He glanced at Ian with a look of incredulity on his face and then stumbled back to the Mercedes and drove off.

Ian flopped back on to the verge, exhausted, gasping for breath, soaking wet and covered in blood.

Despite it being a busy road, at 8.00 PM on a Friday night nothing had passed for the duration of the fight until now when a husband and wife driving a small family car approached from the direction of Harrogate and saw the carnage of the abandoned E-type with Ian lying on the verge. They pulled over and ran to the body.

Referring to a row of terraced cottages a little further up the road, the wife turned to her husband, "Run to one of those houses and ask them to call an ambulance. He's still alive."

Chapter Eighteen

August 1987 – London

Frederick had driven to Ripon Hospital and a surprised nurse had quickly arranged for an ambulance to take him to Leeds General Infirmary where they had the specialist skills necessary to deal with his injury.

The difficulty had been to prevent him choking on his own blood as there is a large blood supply to the mouth and his tongue was bleeding profusely. In the ambulance, the paramedics kept his head down and tried to calm his obvious distress. However, the injury was not as bad as it appeared. Using a saw, a surgeon removed the base of the pen from below Frederick's chin. He then removed a central section of the blade, between the floor of the mouth and the underside of the tongue. This allowed him to pull the bottom section up through the jaw. The surgeon then released the upper section from the roof of the mouth and pulled it up through the tongue. It was then simply a matter of stitching the wound and providing painkillers.

Given the nature of the wound, the hospital had called the police. Frederick played on his swollen tongue to try to avoid answering questions until he could call his lawyer and then claimed he was the victim of a road rage attack but after speaking with Ian, who gave a much more detailed account of the evening's events, Frederick was charged with attempted murder.

Ian had been taken to Harrogate Hospital. He thought it rather ironic given that this was where the whole saga with John Field had started. He was stripped and sponged down by a nurse so she could see how serious his wounds were. X-rays showed his right ankle was broken but thanks to his muscle-mass his left leg was not. However, such was the extent of the bruising, the entire leg turned completely black and was so stiff Ian was hardly able to bend it. The cuts just needed a few stitches, but they kept him in overnight to check for concussion.

All this information had been relayed to Rebecca Topping by the Foreign Secretary on Sunday evening following the accident and now on Monday morning she stormed into MI6 headquarters and asked Jane to send Simon Black to see her.

Rebecca Topping was one of the deputy chiefs of MI6 and as head of the Western European Department, she was responsible for Simon Black. Oxford-educated, she had a brilliant mind, but she was also a prima donna, had to get her own way and was petulant when she didn't. Also, she had a habit of treating her colleagues like children and her mood could swing from being open and friendly to sulky and severe if something was said that met with her disapproval.

Black disliked her intensely and made little attempt to hide his feelings. He didn't like the fact that she was a socialist yet privately educated her children and used a private health clinic on Harley Street. He didn't like the fact that she eschewed exercise to the extent that she belittled all sports and went outside as little as possible. Most of all, however, he found it extremely irritating that she was a woman at the top of her tree who insisted on being the star of the show.

Black walked into her office and sat down without being asked. Topping was standing behind her desk, rifling through her briefcase. She pulled out some newspapers and threw them on the desk in front of him.

"Look at these headlines!"

Black had already savoured them over breakfast, but he flicked through them to amuse her. She read some out.

"Bank on the Brink."

"Frederick Granville charged with attempted murder."

"Lord Granville's Nazi past revealed."

"The Foreign Secretary's spitting blood," she screamed.

"He's not the only one, so I understand," Black said, referring to Frederick's injury.

"That's in poor taste."

Black didn't reply so Topping continued.

"How did they get all this information?" Topping shouted, pointing towards the newspapers.

"I assume the police briefed them."

Topping had a round, smiley face, shoulder-length brown hair and usually a "Daddy's little princess" demeanour but now her face was firmly fixed, and she gave Black her "I wasn't born yesterday" look.

"The police would inform the Press of the car accident and of the fact that Frederick Granville had been charged with attempted murder. They would not know that his father was an SS officer or that Granville's bank had funded the Nazi party."

"Perhaps Sutherland told them?"

"Don't give me that. I know all about your background."

Black took that as an insult. His personnel file would reveal that he was a refugee, but she had no idea what he had suffered.

"You know nothing about me," he snapped.

"I know enough to realise that you have manipulated the truth and used this Service for your own purposes."

"Prove it. The record will show that I have had one interview with Sutherland, which was perfectly proper and fully minuted. Hatchett and Meeks were the ones that spoke to Frederick Granville. I've never met him and was not privy to their conversation. It's just a pity that newspapers never reveal their sources," he said sarcastically.

"I don't care what the record shows. You have brought the Secret Intelligent Service into disrepute. Do you think the Government wants another scandal? Do you think the Bank of England wants a run on Granville's bank? You've engineered a crisis when you're meant to prevent them. I want your resignation by the end of the day."

Black relaxed and smiled at her in a patronising way. He was ten years older than her and enjoyed making her feel like his pupil even though she held the senior position. He knew she had no evidence, or she would have used it. She had nothing on him, and she couldn't force him to do anything.

"I'm not going during a period of media scrutiny. That would give the wrong impression about my departure. I will retire on 31st March 1989 – in 18 months."

Topping scoffed. She couldn't bear the arrogance of the man and this was her chance to be rid of him.

"What makes you think you can dictate terms? I know you're behind this and the Foreign Secretary wants your head - preferably on a silver platter."

Black smiled again.

"My dear lady. Tell the Foreign Secretary that I have given my adult life to this Service and I feel it would be prudent if I tied up a few loose ends before I leave. It would be most unfortunate if there were further leaks because I had been unable to do so." Black's words dripped with condescension.

Topping fired straight back at him. "That's blackmail."

"Not at all. I'm simply being judicious."

Topping stared at Black in silence and then picked up the telephone and dialled her secretary.

"Type out a resignation letter for Simon Black and date it, 31st March 1989," and then turning to Black she said: "I want this signing today before you leave the office."

After the meeting with Simon Black, Rebecca Topping called for Tom Meeks and if she had been angry before she was now seething.

"Tell me your part in this," she barked at him when he entered her office.

"We picked up Sutherland at the airport on 21st August and brought him in for questioning. Then on 28th August, Mr Black said Sutherland had been to see him the previous day and said he was going to tell his story to the Press, so Mr Black asked us to attend Frederick Granville and forewarn him."

"Wait a minute. Are you telling me there was a second meeting?"

"I believe so."

"Then why doesn't the file show that?"

"I have no idea," Meeks responded with a sardonic smile.

Topping didn't like Meeks' attitude. He was too relaxed.

"And you didn't think Black's request unusual?" Her

voice was rising.

"Not really; not for him. Look, if you want to find a chink in his armour ask him how Sutherland knew Granville's bank was financing the Nazi party."

"Why didn't you ask him?"

"I did but he brushed it off."

"And you did nothing about it?"

"Above my pay grade. It's not for me to question the ethics."

"Well, yes, it is actually. Your first duty is to uphold the integrity of the Service, yet despite knowing something was amiss, you chose to ignore it."

Meeks looked startled and sat up in his chair. For the first time during this meeting, he was concerned.

"I don't think there was much I could have done." The words tumbled from his lips.

"You could have come to see me. The fact that you didn't shows a weakness of character that I'm afraid makes you unsuitable for a career in the Secret Intelligence Service." Topping paused while she watched Meeks' face fall in shock. "You're entitled to three months' notice, but we'll pay you until the end of the year. Now, go and clear your desk and send Hatchett in before you leave the premises."

"But I've got a mortgage to pay and two children." Meeks had been taken completely by surprise and was almost begging.

"I'm sure you will find something," she said curtly. "Good-bye."

Meeks walked out of the room and Topping sighed with relief. She didn't like sacking people, but Meeks gave her the head she needed now that Black's was unavailable, and, in any case, she thought he was pathetic.

Hatchett knocked on Topping's door and burst in without waiting. He had just been briefed by Meeks and was worried about his own position.

"I'm not taking the rap for this. This was Black's baby."

"Sit down," Topping replied firmly. "You obviously have your concerns that protocol wasn't followed?"

"Well, I've just spoken with Meeks and can't believe he's been sacked."

"He was expendable and you're going to have to show me you're not. Now, what didn't you like about this assignment?"

"I thought it went beyond the usual scope of what an Operational Officer is supposed to do. We are meant to collect intelligence. In this case, we were being asked to reveal intelligence to a third party."

"So why did you do it?"

"Because Black said I had to look at the bigger picture. He said he was retiring soon, and I needed to step up my game if I was going to replace him."

"So, you compromised your position for the sake of

your career?"

"No!" Hatchett stood up and started pacing from side to side, flinging his arms about as he spoke. "It wasn't like that. I thought, maybe, he was right."

"You had your doubts, but you chose to ignore them for the sake of your career." Topping repeated the accusation to show the argument hadn't been won.

"Okay, yes, maybe there's something in that," Hatchett shouted, throwing his arms in the air.

"Sit down," Topping growled. "You're aggressive, volatile and inconsistent. However, you may have your uses."

Hatchett sat down, looking rather sheepish and Topping continued.

"Black is going to retire in 18 months and I do need someone to replace him, so you are going to have to keep your head down and do exactly as your told. Do you understand?"

"Yes," Hatchett nodded with relief.

"Can I rely on your loyalty? Black is going to need watching carefully until he leaves and then I want to reshape the whole department."

"Yes, I have no special allegiance to Black. I don't trust him."

"Good. Well, the first thing I want you to do is to go and speak with Ian Sutherland. We owe him an apology. You owe him an apology. See if you can find out what he intends to do. I'm hoping he will exercise his discretion and not mention our involvement, although he will have to give evidence when Frederick Granville faces trial. This is a delicate situation. Show me how you can handle it."

"Yes, ma'am. When would you like me to go?" Hatchett's relief was turning into enthusiasm.

Topping looked at her watch. It was nearly lunchtime.

"Tomorrow. And let me know what happens."

Chapter Nineteen

September 1987 – Harrogate

Ian had been discharged from hospital on Sunday morning but not before Beth had discovered he was there and come to see him.

"You never called me," she said, looking disappointed.

"No, sorry," Ian replied. "I've been busy."

She looked pretty but seeing her again only re-affirmed his feelings for Sophie.

He had taken the Monday off work to sort out the repairs to the E-type, which was not too badly damaged and to see if he could claim for his suit on his house insurance because it was completely ruined.

He walked to work on Tuesday morning. The doctor had said it was important to keep moving and he obviously couldn't drive with a pot on his right foot, not to mention the fact he didn't have a car!

It took longer than he thought. He had discarded the crutches given to him by the hospital and was relying on a walking stick, which helped take some of the strain off his legs while providing stability. The broken ankle was easy for him to comprehend and encased in plaster, it was not giving him too much discomfort. The left leg, however, was black. Not purple or showing multi-coloured bruising, but completely black and it was causing him some pain.

Ian knew he would be fine in a few weeks, and he wanted to downplay his injuries because he had telephoned Sophie and she was flying over to be with him. She had been quite indignant on his behalf when he spoke to her, so he wanted to look his best and not worry her unnecessarily.

Hannah Ryder was the first to say something. She put her head round his door and smiled sympathetically.

"I didn't think you would be in so soon. Are you all right?"

"Yes, I'm fine, thank you."

"From all the Press reports, it sounds as though you've had quite a dramatic holiday?"

"Yes, it was somewhat, but it is all sorted now."

"Good, well, let me know if you need anything. We can have a proper chat later."

Ian was just thinking how lovely she was when Ronnie Roberts bowled through his door.

"So, you're back, are you?"

Ian looked at himself to check he was there.

"It seems so," he replied, a little sarcastically.

"Good, well, I'm glad you're all right, but…" He paused and lowered his voice, "at Ryders we don't seek publicity. Not really Cricket to self-promote oneself."

"Sorry," Ian said. "I'll try to remember that next time I'm run over."

Ian was rescued from the awkwardness of the situation by a telephone call from Sarah on reception.

"There's a Mr Hatchett here to see you."

"That's odd," Ian replied. "He hasn't got an appointment, but I'll come down."

Ian took Hatchett into one of the meeting rooms. Rather than the clinical sterility of the MI6 offices, Ryders' meeting rooms were warmly furnished with thick carpets, mahogany furniture and historical paintings on the walls. Ian had chosen meeting room number two as this eschewed the formality of the board room and had some Chippendale-style armchairs arranged around a broad, low coffee table. Hatchett looked around and Ian could see he was impressed.

"Would you like some coffee?"

"Yes please," Hatchett responded enthusiastically and by the way he demolished the rather ordinary choice of biscuits, Ian suspected he must have had an early start to his day. He had a bit of a hang-dog expression on his face and once the pleasantries were over, he asked, "How are you?"

"I'm fine. I have a broken ankle and some bruising, but I'll be fighting fit in a few weeks."

Hatchett was looking at Ian and nodding.

"Frederick Granville is still in jail and we don't think he will get bail."

"Good. I don't want to bump into him again," Ian chuckled but Hatchett didn't seem to get the pun.

"Meeks has been sacked."

"Really?" Ian interrupted a little surprised. He hadn't really thought of Meeks as a key player in this story.

"I think he's the official scapegoat. Black is retiring but not for 18 months."

"Why are MI6 taking the blame? It was Frederick Granville who attacked me although I'm still not sure why."

"I think it might have something to do with the fact that we told him you were going to the Press. I think he was worried you were going to ruin his bank and the family's reputation."

"What!" Ian exclaimed. "Simon Black asked me to go to the Press, but I refused."

Hatchett stared at his size 12 feet. He was looking guilty.

"We suspected that might be the case. I've been sent to apologise on behalf of the Service and I'm sorry for my part in it too," he said struggling to overcome his pride.

"That's okay. It's over now," Ian said, giving a typically British response.

"There will be a trial, of course, and you will have to give evidence, but the Service normally prides itself on discretion so we hope you can keep any references to MI6 to the minimum."

"Understood," Ian replied, now realising the purpose of the meeting.

Ian limped to the front door, said good-bye to Hatchett and as he came back through reception, Sarah handed him a small envelope.

"This has just been delivered for you," she said as though it had caused her a great inconvenience.

"Thank you," Ian said as he went back to his office to open it.

The envelope contained a notelet with a rather sophisticated drawing of Athena on the front. It was from Simon Black asking Ian to meet him for a coffee at noon, at a café nearby, called The Met.

Ian looked at his watch. He'd got half an hour. Then he looked at the picture again and turned to the back of the notelet. The description confirmed that the image was of Athena, goddess of wisdom and war.

He's got a nerve, Ian thought, but I might as well go and see what he has to say for himself.

Sophie was hoping to get to Harrogate around lunchtime and was going to come straight to the office, so Ian asked Sarah to say he had been called to a meeting and suggest they meet up at Bettys at 1.00 PM; a request to which she reluctantly agreed. He then hobbled to The Met which was a basement café underneath a hairdresser's salon. It was also owned by the hairdresser and had the same ground floor entrance as the salon, so Ian had to weave his way past a cordon of elderly ladies and negotiate some rather steep stairs to the basement.

The air was humid from the hot water and hair dryers and stale from the lack of circulation. Ian immediately felt uncomfortable and as he went down the stairs, sideways, dropping his left leg, one step at a time, he wondered why Black would choose such a location. Then he realised that stuck underground behind the blue-rinse brigade, no one was going to notice them.

Simon Black rose to greet him and proffered his hand.

"My dear chap, how are you?"

"I'm fine," Ian said, shaking his hand.

"What would you like to drink?"

"Just some water please," Ian said, running his finger around the inside of his collar. He was overly warm and had just had coffee with Hatchett.

Black watched as Ian sat down rather awkwardly with his left leg stretched out straight and his face straining as he threw his weight on to the walking stick.

"I'm relieved to see you are not too badly injured. I was worried when I heard you had been run over."

Ian wondered if it was relief at not being responsible for more serious injuries, but it was not. Black seemed to have a genuine affection for him.

"Well, it will take more than a psycho in a Mercedes to

stop me." Ian heard himself say these words and thought they sounded silly, but this boyish bravado was the first thing that came into his head.

"Yes, I understand Frederick Granville is a nasty piece of work. Prison is the best place for him."

"What will happen to the bank?"

"We will have to wait and see but a snake can't strike without its head."

"Is that a quote from something?" Ian asked.

"No, I just made it up," Black said laughing as he did so. "It may just wither on the vine. With Frederick in prison, there is no family member to provide leadership. It will be interesting watching what happens although I don't think *interesting* is the word Lord Granville would use."

"Something for you to enjoy in your retirement, perhaps?" Ian was prodding him now and Black was taken by surprise.

"Word gets around quickly, but 18 months is a long time. Anything could happen between now and then," he replied a little sharply.

"Well, you said you usually get your own way in the end. Maybe, it won't happen."

"Yes, I did say that. It is important to set objectives and then stick to them. If the objective is right, the route is immaterial."

"Even if there is a sacrificial lamb?"

It was Black who was feeling uncomfortable now. Ian's eyes had narrowed, and he was looking straight through him.

"If I could have done things differently, I would have done but time was running against me and I was hopeful that you could handle whatever was thrown at you – even if it was a car." Black laughed at his own joke and started regaining his composure.

"I don't understand why it was so important to you. It seems almost personal."

"You can't know everything, but I had my reasons. I hope this won't come between us?"

"I don't hold grudges," Ian replied.

Black sat back and smiled. "That's what I like about you. You look at things objectively. Throughout this process, you have displayed all those characteristics that attracted me to you in the first place."

There was a time when Ian would have swollen with pride at this comment but now, Black had lost his hold over him. He could see him for what he was, and the comment was simply patronising.

"I've got to go," Ian said, starting the routine of standing up by pushing down on the walking stick.

Black wasn't expecting Ian to leave so suddenly, and he scrambled for some words.

"Well, keep in touch. I may need you again. We're the same, you know."

Ian was almost upright now but perspiring with the effort and pain. He twisted around and looked into Black's eyes.

"No, we're not. You see chess pieces – I see people."

It was a relief to be back outside in the September sunlight and fresh air. Ian breathed it in deeply and left his jacket open as he made his way to Bettys, hoping that the light breeze would make him look less flushed for Sophie.

He saw her immediately, about to sit down at one of the tables, and involuntarily, he took a sharp intake of air.

She had just removed her black leather jacket and placed it over the back of a chair revealing a black lace blouse which she was wearing with a cream, above the knee, leather pencil skirt and black high heels. She looked utterly captivating.

Sophie saw Ian out of the corner of her eye and ran over to him, throwing her arms around his neck, nearly causing him to lose his balance.

"You take my breath away," he whispered.

Sophie stood back to look at him, still holding on to his biceps.

"What have they done to you?"

"I'm okay. I'll soon be back to normal."

They sat at the table and in between glancing at the menu and ordering, they kept touching hands and looking into each other's eyes.

"Is this over now?" Sophie asked. "No more Simon

Black? No more MI6? No more problems?"

"There is just one more problem I have to resolve," Ian said in all seriousness.

"Oh no," Sophie said, her head dropping as though her neck had suddenly lost all its strength. "What now?"

"The distance between Munich and Harrogate is too great. One of us is going to have to move."

Sophie's face broke into a smile and her eyes sparkled. Ian looked at her and was happy.